ONE MINUTE I HATE YOU 3

A HOOD LOVE STORY

LEILANI

One Minute I Hate You 3

Copyright © 2022 by Leilani

All rights reserved.

Published in the United States of America.

Published by Cole Hart Signature, LLC.

Mailing List

To stay up to date on new releases, plus get information on contests, sneak peeks, and more,

Go To The Website Below...

www.colehartsignature.com

CHAPTER ONE
ZACHARY "ZOO" SLAID
NEXT DAY

The sun was out, birds chirped, and the smell of freshly cut grass and boiled peanuts filled the stadium. The Braves were down by three and it was the last inning. The fans were on edge because we had two outs and the bases were loaded. All we needed was one good hit to send everybody in.

"Wooohooo," Ryah cheered.

I put my arm around her and pulled her over to me. I took in her vanilla scent, wishing I could live in that moment forever. "What's wrong? You okay?" She pulled my dreads back. "Something's bothering you," she continued.

"Nah, I'm good," I lied.

She knew I was lying too. Zaryah could look through a muthafucka's soul. I had too much on me to ruin the moment though. I had big plans for her but my mind kept wandering off. Skyler springing Hero on me had my mind completely fucked up. I had just got back good with Ryah. Then she had the nerve to tell me I couldn't see him because I asked for a DNA test. She was foul as fuck.

I called Ro last night to tell him how I went from a free man to daddy's daycare overnight, but he didn't answer. I even hit his line twice before the game and he didn't answer or respond. Something in my gut told me something was wrong, but I shook it off and continued to kick shit with my lady.

"Strike three, the Chicago Cubs win!" the spokesperson yelled over the mic.

All of the home team fans sighed in unison, even Ryah. I had barely paid attention to anything that had happened the entire game. I would tune in when Ryah spoke to me, but my mind kept wandering off to the Skyler and Hero situation. *How? One nut and she gets pregnant again? What are the fucking odds?*

Snapping out of my thoughts, I gave Ryah my attention. "Oh, so you feeling the Braves, huh?"

"Yeah, I didn't think I would enjoy it this much," she said.

"Well, I'm glad you did, ma. I have more in store for you," I said with a wink.

She smiled and grabbed me by the hand so we could leave. I felt guilty as fuck. I had yet another secret kid. *Damn.* But everything that I was doing, was out of love. I wanted Ryah to feel special. I didn't want her to think I was spoiling her out of guilt. But that wouldn't matter, 'cause I knew it was gon' be hell anyways when I told her about Hero.

I put that shit in the back of my head and continued on to the car with her. She was glowing from head to toe. Her skin was flawless, body was banging, and the energy was good. She was genuinely happy and that shit made me feel good. I couldn't fuck up my fairytale just yet. I had to hold on just a little longer.

We pulled into my neighborhood and I had Ryah cover her eyes.

"Why do I have to close my eyes?" she whined.

"You'll see."

When we got to my house I told her to uncover her eyes. And the look on her face was priceless. She shook her head from side to side as I handed her the keys to her new white Range Rover. She covered her mouth in excitement.

"I don't deserve this," she said.

She was on the brink of tears, with her soft ass. "Baby, you deserve the world. I just haven't found out how to give it to you yet," I said.

And that's when the waterworks came. She wrapped her arms around my neck and hugged me for damn near twenty minutes. I had to pry her off of me so she could check out her new whip. In my twenty-seven years of living, I had never had a woman be so grateful, so humble. My shawty said she didn't deserve it. Any other bitch would've snatched the keys and thought no more about it.

She hopped on the driver's side and squealed over and over. She was in disbelief. That's how I knew I did good.

"You wanna take it for a spin while Jase is still with his people?"

Or maybe I should've said *our* people, since my auntie Carla and her husband had him. It's crazy because both of them wanted nothing to do with me or Ryah. I could understand why they didn't care for me since I almost put my unc in a wheelchair from that ass whooping. But Ryah had nothing to do with that shit.

Carla was just pissed at Ryah because of what happened with Kareem. I told Ryah to find a babysitter for the day because I had something special for her. Auntie Carla showed her ass when Ryah called her. The only way she would watch Jase was if Ryah dropped him off at Ma Duke's house and she picked him after we left, crazy.

"Did you hear me, bae?"

Snapping out of my train of thought, I looked at Ryah to see what she was saying to me. She patted the seat with a smile and told me to come on. She could hardly contain herself. It was a gift to see the happiness plastered over her face.

"Are you sure you're okay, bae? You've been kinda out of it since the game," she said.

Ryah was good at noticing when something was off. Shorty could look through souls, and that made me even more nervous. Mama always said, "a guilty conscience never feels secure." I think she read that shit in a book or something. She always had a wise saying for every situation.

"I'm good, ma. Put this bitch in sports mode and let's see how you driving now," I said.

She studied me a little more before sticking the key in the ignition. She had a worried look on her face, but she dropped it and continued on to celebrate. We drove all over Atlanta in the new ride. It was lit. I loved to see her hair blow in the wind. That shit was sexy as fuck. I had one more surprise for her, so I told her to pull over into a nearby parking garage.

"Zoo, what more could you possibly have for me?" She smiled. "You're gonna end up spoiling me if you keep giving me princess treatment."

"Baby, I'mma give you everything your heart desires. I told you that. Now, close your eyes," I said.

I reached into the dashboard and grabbed a box that held the key to my house inside. I wanted Ryah and Jase to move in with me. I didn't want her ass to work, struggle, sweat, none of that shit. After all the hell that she had been through, she deserved nothing more than to sit up in a young rich nigga's mini-mansion with her feet up.

I told her to open her eyes, and I opened the box at the same time. "A key?"

"The key to my place. I want you and Jase to move in with

me. No more twelve-hour shifts and no more struggling to make ends meet. Let me take care of y'all."

She fell silent. I could tell by her facial expression I wasn't about to get the answer I wanted. She took the key and held it to her heart.

"All of that sounds amazing, but I can't do that, Zoo. At least not right now. After everything with Kareem, I learned a lot. I still love you and I still wanna be with you, but we can't move in with you right now. I'm pacing myself. Jase still hasn't healed from all of the emotional scars from his father. We both need time," she said in a tone a little above a whisper.

She expected me to be upset, but I wasn't at all. She needed time and I could give her that. We were still good, so that's all that mattered. Respect goes a long way in a relationship. I knew we were always good as long as we had respect. I told her to hold onto the key since it was hers anyways.

"I love you too, woman. I'd wait a hunnid years for you."

She smiled and kissed my lips. I felt myself becoming aroused and I hoped to God that she would let me play in that pussy. I hadn't felt pussy since I fucked Lenoir way back when. My dick was hard as steel and the print in my jeans made that known.

Her eyes fell to my manhood, and she licked her full lips from corner to corner. I freed the beast, causing a smirk to cross her face. She leaned over the armrest and positioned her mouth on my dick. She slowly sucked the head while caressing my balls. Her mouth felt like Heaven. I had to clench my cheeks together to keep from busting so quickly.

Then, rising up, she let a glob of spit drip from her mouth onto the tip. She used her right hand to caress my shit and used her left hand to choke me. That shit was so fucking sexy, I couldn't help but nut quick.

"Fuckkk, ma!" I let out a breath and my chest heaved up

and down. "What the fuck are you doing to me, girl? You gon' make me crazy," I continued.

I bit down on my bottom lip and admired every feature about her beautiful ass. "Do you want me?" she asked.

She wore a cute lil' pink leather skirt that gave me all the access I needed. She slid her blue thong over to the side, revealing her shaved pussy. It was leaking for me. My eyes were fixated on the very thing I was hungry for. I laid the seat back.

"Come sit that pussy on my face, girl."

She climbed over the seat and maneuvered her way onto my mouth. I flickered my tongue across her pearl as she grinded her hips. I clamped down softly on her clit and with the tip of my tongue, I found that tiny little spot that women loved. And the moment the tip of my tongue touched it, it was as if a bolt of lightning hit her. She almost smothered a nigga.

That didn't stop the beast though. I sucked and slurped on her clit until my fingers came into play. I inserted two fingers into her pink pussy, causing her to soak the collar of my shirt and the head of the seat. I pumped my fingers in and out of her.

"Shit! Daddy!... Fuck!"

She squirmed and moaned out in pleasure. That shit turned me on even more. I was intoxicated by her, I couldn't get enough. My tongue needed that pussy, and I didn't let up until her honey flowed into my mouth and down my throat. And what I missed ran down my cheeks.

She climbed from my face and back to her seat. Then she freed my hard dick. It was sticky with more cum. I raised my hips and slid my pants and boxers down to my knees. She dropped her head to my lap and went to work again. I involuntarily shouted her name as she throated my shit all the way down to my pubic hair. Her long tongue wrapped itself around my dick and she sucked me until I was weak. I was in another world of pleasure.

But the best was yet to come. She climbed back over the console, facing me, with her back to the dashboard. She lowered herself on my rock-hard dick, and I couldn't help but moan out. Her pussy was warm and tight. She stared me in the eyes, and I swear I could feel my soul leave my body. We were fused together, a single body.

I sucked on her nipples as she bounced up and down. I could feel her pussy contracting. She flung her head back and grabbed onto my neck. She tightened her grip, slightly choking me but turning me on even more. I grabbed her by the waist and rammed her harder onto my dick. My hips thrusted, giving her blow for blow.

"Fuckkkkkkkk!" I moaned as I nutted.

My chest heaved up and down. We were both panting like we'd run a marathon. Ryah was laid over me, out of breath and sweaty as fuck. The windows were all fogged up. I couldn't see shit. I wanted to lay in that moment forever and forget about stuff I had going on in my life. Ryah deserved to know the truth. So I decided to tell her right then and there about Hero. Shawty fucked the truth out of me.

"Sit up, baby. Let me talk to you," I said.

Bzzt. Bzzt. Bzzt. Grabbing my vibrating phone from the floor, I glanced over the screen. The salon was calling, and they hardly ever called, unless there was some kind of problem. I swiped the green circle to the right and placed the phone to my ear.

"Yo."

"Zoo, Ro never came by here. I've been calling him and blowing him up but he ain't answering. Have you talked to him? You know he doesn't miss load day."

I hurriedly sat up. I put Ryah to the side and pulled my

pants up over my ass. She was right. Ro had never missed a load day.

"Aite. I'm about to call him now," I said.

I called Ro's phone multiple times and got nothing. I hit Chip's line to see if he had heard from him, but he said he had been trying to reach him too.

"Aye, call Mara real quick and see if she heard from Ro," I said to Ryah.

"Mara ain't fucking with me like that. It's been a minute since I've talked to her," she said.

"What? Why?"

"I don't really wanna get into it. We just need a break from each other. That's all." She straightened her clothes as she spoke. "You don't think anything happened, do you?"

"I don't know. But something ain't right. I still need you to call, bae."

Picking up her phone, she called Kamara back to back and got no answer from her either. We switched positions, and I got on the driver's side while she rode the passenger. Something didn't feel right. When Ryah called Kamara's mother and she hadn't heard from her, she was nervous too.

The first place I went was their house. Ryah almost jumped out of the moving car when she saw yellow tape and police cars everywhere. It felt like everything was moving in slow motion. The blue and red lights flashed, officers walked in and out of the house, and there was so much chatter that it felt like echoes in my head.

Cones were set up everywhere. They had the perimeter taped off from the public. All of the neighbors were outside looking around. Blood was everywhere. There was a trail from the house through the driveway. That amount of blood was never a good sign.

Ryah pulled my arm, bringing me back to reality. "We have

to get to the hospital now! They said that two people were shot multiple times and they were transported to the hospital!" she wailed.

"Fuckkkk!" I clenched my fists in anger. "I'm so tired of these fucking hospitals!"

I was too shaken to even drive. Ryah drove and on the way there, she called Kamara's mama to let her know what was going on. I wish I knew somebody to call for Ro, but he didn't really have anybody. His OG was all cracked up just like mine, so she was a lost cause.

I think that's why we clicked so well. His pops was alive and well, but they had no type of relationship. When Ro's OG got into the streets hard, that nigga dipped and left them for dead. Ro had to man up and take care of himself and a crack-head at the tender age of fourteen. His bitch-ass daddy started an entirely new family and Ro hadn't talked to him since we were back in high school. And as far as his moms, last I heard, she got a hold to some bad drugs and it fucked up her mental.

Somebody laced her shit and Ro had to put her in a facility. The closest thing he had to a real sibling was me. I mean, his pops had other kids, but we didn't know them fools, so there's that. Ro never fucked with any extended family like cousins, aunts, or uncles. Family had always been a touchy subject for him. He never really got into it. But I didn't have time to run ancestry and DNA tests through the hood. I was all the family my boy needed.

"They're going to be okay," Ryah said, placing her hand on top of mine.

I hadn't even realized that we had made it to the hospital. I was so busy going down memory lane. We unclicked our seat-belts and headed inside to the emergency room department. The first nurse we spotted, we asked her for any information she had on Romeo Walton and Kamara Wade. She directed us to the nurses' station and a short little blonde girl searched them in the system.

"Give me one moment while I grab the doctor," she said.

My anxiety was through the roof. Kamara's mama ended up showing up while we were waiting for the doctor. She looked like she had been crying her entire drive here. Ryah consoled her and patted her on the back as they comforted each other.

"Are you all the family of Wade and Walton?" an Indian doctor asked.

We all rushed over to her to see what the news was. "Yes, we are the family," Kamara's mother said.

"Very well. Mr. Walton sustained three shots to the chest, two striking major organs and the other sitting on the spine. He's in critical condition and he needs surgery as soon as possible in order for him to walk again. The holdup for surgery is because of his other injuries. It will be too risky to perform surgery with his condition, death will likely follow. We plan to monitor him closely for the next three days and if he's stable enough, we will remove the bullet pressed against his spine."

"And what about Kamara Wade?" Her mother was so anxious, she was shaking.

"Ms. Wade was shot five times, including one shot to the head." Ms. Wade broke down to the ground and Ryah grabbed her. The doctor knelt down beside them to comfort her too. "Kamara is in very critical condition. The bullet pierced the skull, penetrating certain parts of her brain. We have done all we can for her and the likelihood of survival is slim to none. We will keep her comfortable. But in the meantime, it's best for you to prepare yourselves for the inevitable."

Ryah grabbed her chest and vomited everywhere when the doctor gave us the news. I tried to pick her up but I could barely keep myself composed. Ms. Wade completely lost it. She wouldn't accept it.

"No! No! No! I won't take that! No! You have to go back and save her!" she shouted to the doctor.

She grabbed onto her white jacket and begged her to fix her daughter. A bypassing nurse had to pry her off of the lady.

"Pleaseeeee! I'm begging you, please. Don't give up on my baby."

Her cries echoed throughout the hallways. Ryah stayed next to her and they cried on the floor while I stood in complete disbelief. *This shit can't be really happening.*

CHAPTER TWO
KAREEM "REEM" BANKS

It's amazing how much time you have to think to yourself when you're locked away in the pits below Hell. Yeah, I said it right, this place was beyond hell. I didn't know how I fucked up my life so badly, but I did. Life was tough and it was only getting worse. If I wasn't haunted by the nightmares of Quesha at night, the guilt of my daughters weighed down on me.

Usually the drugs would drown all of those thoughts away but the withdrawals was another demon I was facing. I was a complete mess. And my stomach still hadn't healed from them fucking rats either. Life as I knew it was over. I wanted to give up. I tried to give up, but my kids. I couldn't give up on myself without still trying to find the whereabouts of my daughter. And I wanted my son to know I was sorry.

But I knew those were issues that would have to be dealt with later. Apparently, word got around the prison pretty quickly about me kidnapping a kid. Niggas had been on my ass since word got out. These boys were dirty. They only let me shower twice a week. Most times, I had to sneak and take bird baths in the sink in the cell. I couldn't imagine what would happen if they found out I was a snitch too. They'd kill me instantly.

"This can't be life," I said aloud.

I wasn't speaking to anyone in particular, but Macho decided to chime in. Every once in a while, he got chatty.

"At least you won't be living for much longer," he said in a sarcastic tone.

I positioned myself upward on the bunk to face him. "What you mean?"

"Them niggas gon' kill you soon."

His face was straight and he didn't move a muscle. Oh, he was serious. "Look man, I can't die here. I still have to find my kid and I still have to make shit right all where I wronged. I can't die, man. I need you to protect me or sum. I'll look out for you," I bargained.

"Heh, you can't look out for me, you can barely take care of yourself. And you better sleep with one eye open. You fucked with a kid and they gon' kill you for that. There's nothing I can do for you, young blood."

And then it clicked. Right when the words left his mouth, an entire plan formed in my head. *Blood.* I needed protection, and who better to get protection from other than a gang? I immediately got myself together the best way I could. I wrapped a shirt around the bottom portion of my face so only my eyes were visible. I did that so it would be harder for niggas to recognize me.

What I was about to do was risky, but I had no other choice. A man will do some crazy shit when his back is up against the wall. And that included trying to join one of the most feared gangs in the south for protection. I went exactly to the spot I knew they posted at, B-block.

Bloods were all about their respect. I knew not to directly

approach them, so I stopped a few feet from the picnic table they sat on. I raised both of my arms to show them that I posed no threat, and I told them I wanted in.

A few of them laughed. The head nigga in charge sat directly in the middle. He didn't find shit funny. He placed his hand in the air and they immediately stopped laughing. He slid from the table and approached me. I had bullets of sweat formed on my forehead. I tried my hardest not to let the fear show.

He snatched the shirt tied to my face. "Ain't you the same nigga on charges for kidnapping a kid?" he questioned me.

I gulped, but I stood tall when I answered him. "Niggas don't have the whole backstory for real."

"Yeah? Well how about this. You tell us the backstory and if you're lying or yo' story ain't good enough, I'mma kill you where you stand. But if your story checks out, we may talk business."

I had no plans of telling him the full story or telling him Zoo's name. Zoo had so much pull, I was scared to mention anything about him to anyone. Crossing Zoo was like crossing East Atlanta. Everybody fucked with him.

But to keep the pressure down, I partially told him the story and left out the part about me snitching. The only thing they needed to know was that a nigga killed my daughter in a fire and I kidnapped his kid in retaliation.

I told him that he could research the story about my daughter online. And that's what they did, too, on the spot. One of his boys pulled the story ASAP and they read over it.

"Heh, an article about your daughter dying proves nothing but you had a motive. Whose kid did you snatch? We need to do some further digging," one of the guys suggested.

Then the leader held his hand up again. "Nah. No need for

that." He laughed. "He could be useful. You wanna be Blood right? Blood in, blood out," he said.

"You want me to kill somebody?"

"Not just anybody, a guard. In order to earn respect and a place at our table, I need a body that means something to drop. You have two weeks."

CHAPTER THREE
ZARYAH "RYAH" COX
NEXT DAY AT THE HOSPITAL

My head felt like someone had repeatedly beat me with a hammer. My tear ducts couldn't form any more tears because they were dried from all the crying I had done all night. The bags around my puffy eyes proved the exhaustion I was going through. Some more of Kamara's family members showed up throughout the night. They took it hard too.

All night long, Kamara's mom, Zoo, and I stayed up praying for a miracle. But the only news we got was terrible since the time we arrived. Kamara's numbers kept dropping all night and nurses and doctors were back and forth in the room. They had her entire head wrapped up, so I could barely see my best friend at all. Only small portions from her face were visible.

I held onto her hand and apologized to her a thousand times for our fight, just hoping that maybe she could hear me. Her body was cold, like it was empty. There was no sense of life in her anymore. I could feel my best friend slipping away and there was nothing we could do for her.

Ms. Wade cried in agony last night every time Mara coded.

I couldn't bear to even look at her in that state. We all felt so helpless. Zoo held onto me through the night for support. I sobbed in his arms, leaving his shirt a mess with snot, tears, and slob. I was a wreck. It didn't feel real, none of it. Just a few months ago my life was normal. The only problem I had was taking care of a nigga that wasn't shit.

I didn't know what to expect anymore. My heart was broken, my friend was suffering, and the last time we talked was when we had an argument. It wasn't supposed to end like that.

Knock. Knock. Mara's doctor knocked on the door before coming in. Her nurse and a woman in a dress followed behind her too, closing the door behind them. The lady in the dress spoke first.

"Good morning, everyone, my name is Chelsea. I'm a social worker here at the hospital. Do you all mind if we speak to Ms. Wade alone?" she asked.

"No. They can stay," Ms. Wade spoke up.

"Very well, you may proceed, Doctor," she said, giving her the floor.

"I know this is a difficult time for you all and I wish there was more we could do, but there isn't. Kamara is suffering and her body has no more fight left. I'm sorry to say this, but Kamara will likely pass within the next few hours. We will try to keep her as comfortable as possible during this process. Chelsea will be available for you at any time you need to speak to someone or for any type of resources beneficial to you. Again, I am so sorry, Ms. Wade."

As she spoke, her voice faded out. It sounded like an echo in my head. My ears were ringing. The room felt like it immediately grew hot. It was harder for me to breathe. I was trapped. I couldn't move. I couldn't talk. I was...

"Ryah! Zaryah! Zaryah!" Zoo stood in front of me, holding

both of my arms. He shook me gently back and forth. "Baby, are you okay? I need you to breathe," he continued.

I looked around. Ms. Wade was on the floor with doctors and nurses surrounding her. They had oxygen over her mouth and they shouted out her vitals. Zoo walked me out of the room and out to the hallway. We sat on a nearby bench.

"I, I, I..."

"Shhhh. I got you, baby. I got you." He pulled me into his chest. "Listen to me, I'm going to take you to my place so you can get some rest. You haven't been to sleep in twenty-four hours. I want you to take a shower and then look in my boxer drawer and grab a Percocet ten. That'll help you sleep. I have Ms. Wade's numbers and I'll keep in check with her. And I'll go by my auntie Carla's house and pick up Jase."

"She is not about to let Jase go with you."

"You wanna bet." He licked those thick lips.

I sighed and shook my head. "Okay." He was right. I was exhausted and I needed the rest.

CHAPTER FOUR
LENOIR HOLLIS

Since my last encounter with Zoo, I'd been a busy woman. I had to do a lot of thinking. As hard as I'd tried to fight the urge from thinking about Zoo, it was impossible. The thought of him alone was exhilarating. No man had ever talked to me the way he did, handled me the way he did, or fucked me the way he did. I'd serve that man pussy any way he wanted it, every day of the week.

He just didn't know what he was missing out on. That's why I said, I'd been busy. I made it one of my top priorities to bag this nigga. And the only way to do that, was to become the ultimate package for a street nigga.

After he flexed on me in front of his kids at the fair, I did some major critical thinking. The nigga that I wanted was a big-time drug lord and I was essentially the opp. He would never give me the time of day as long as I wore that badge. So I did what I had to do, I quit.

Yepp, I quit on their ass and cashed out my 401k. But I knew that wouldn't be enough to snatch the nigga of my dreams. I needed more. I needed to be like dumb ass Zaryah

Cox. The dumb-dumb who took the charge for Kareem Banks. And some bitches may think I'm stupid too. But call it what you want. I don't see anything wrong with going after the man I wanted. We had already fucked and he loved my shit. I just needed him to get to know me.

The face card was already giving pretty bitch vibes but the body had to go. I booked a surgery with the money Zoo gave me in that offshore account and I still had some left over. I dropped thirty-five thousand dollars for my body alone. I was excited for the outcome of surgery but I was nervous to go under the knife.

I arrived in Miami over two hours ago and the Uber driver recently dropped me off at the clinic's location. The staff was friendly and welcoming, so that calmed my nerves a little. As I looked around, all of the other women had friends or family alongside them to support them but I had no one. I'd never really been a friendly person. I hung out with the people on the force. I had no outside friends. And my family, Lord, would kill me if they found out I was undergoing cosmetic surgery. I came from a family of heavier set people, so let's just say, that conversation wouldn't go over well with them.

"Lenoir Hollis," a lady with pink scrubs called out.

She stood by the door holding a clipboard and smiling. I put my hand up to let her know that was me. Then I grabbed my belongings and followed her to the back. *You got this, Lenoir. You got this,* I told myself this same chant over and over.

"Are you nervous?" she asked.

I nodded my head. "Oh my goodness, yes. I've tried to stay out of my head about it but I'm so damn scared," I admitted.

"That's normal, darling. Everyone is nervous on their first go around. And the surgeon is bomb, so you're in good hands."

First go around? Oh, this is my only go around. I'm already scared out of my mind. She led me to an office where my surgeon sat behind a big Cherokee desk with pictures of my naked body spread across it. It was kinda disturbing being that he had his kids' picture framed and sitting on his desk as well.

"Miss Hollis, glad you could make it." He smiled.

I greeted him back with a smile and a handshake. Then we got straight to it. He went through each picture individually and went over what changes he was going to make again. His focus was my stomach, hips, and ass. It was the same thing we had discussed over the phone during my telehealth visit.

"Okay. Sounds good," I said.

"Great. I just need your signature on a few more documents and my nurse will get you ready for pre-op."

"Okay." And just like that, I officially ran up a check on my body. It was exciting and nerve racking at the same time. I didn't know what to expect. I read plenty of great reviews after having surgery but, of course, there were the extremely scary ones too.

But I tried to stay out of my head about it. We went to the back and let all the magic happen.

* * *

AFTER SURGERY

After surgery was everything I imagined it to be. I knew it would be painful, so I tried to prepare myself the best way I could. It wasn't an aching pain though. It was a burning pain. My body was on fire. It hurt to touch anywhere.

The second I opened my eyes, I felt it. The surgeon was only here for ten minutes to educate me on the aftercare. He gave me a mirror and showed me my new sculpted body. It was amazing. He bodied me for real. No bitch was fucking with me.

The surgeon left and the rest was left in the hands of the nurses. I was smart and paid for the recovery stay at the hotel connected to the hospital. I knew I would be in too much pain to care for myself after surgery, so I spent five thousand extra dollars for the post-op care.

"Okay, my dear, my name is Sophie and I'll be your recovery nurse for your stay. You can follow me to your room and there you will have all of the aftercare necessities that we discussed. You know, like the compression garment that you'll need to wear for eight hours a day and your sitting pillow. After a few days of post-op, you'll notice a lot of swelling in areas of your body. Don't worry, that's normal. The massages that you'll get throughout the day will help with the swelling. And I can tell by your face that you're a little uneasy. Listen, we will make your stay here as comfy and easy as possible. And at the end, I promise it'll all be worth it."

I smiled. She was right. The end goal was to make Zoo my man. Surgery was a minor snag I had to get through. And they didn't leave me completely hanging. They gave me pain pills to take around the clock.

Sophie led me to my room and it was nothing like what I expected. It looked exactly like a nice hotel room, besides the hospital bed. They really set me up nicely. I walked over to the full-body mirror and admired my new figure. I went from a size twenty to a size thirteen quickly.

"You look amazing. And you'll be even more perfect after recovery," Sophie complimented.

I warmed her with a smile. "Thank you. I can't wait."

"Of course. I see that you came from Georgia." She pulled back the covers of the bed. "Anyone special back home waiting for the new Lenoir?"

She was cute, a little nosey but she meant no harm. The

small talk made it less awkward. She even complimented my skin and asked me for my skin regiment.

"Actually, my boyfriend has no idea that I even did this. He's gonna be surprised when I get back to Atlanta," I lied.

Well, it wasn't a complete lie. I knew Zoo would be surprised when he saw me. I just wasn't his girlfriend, yet.

She walked over to me and placed her hands gently on my shoulders from behind. We stared in the mirror together. "Girl, he is going to love this. Take my word. I know." She winked.

This is about to be a long two weeks.

CHAPTER FIVE
ZARYAH "RYAH" COX
1 WEEK LATER

Last week I felt like I was back in prison again. I couldn't eat or sleep. I was falling into depression. Kamara ended up dying within a few hours like the doctors said she would, and I'd been sick ever since. None of it felt real. My homie, my ace boon coon, my dawg, my sister, my best fucking friend was gone. Gone forever. The only peace I'd been able to find was through a Hennessy bottle.

Zoo had been by my side the entire time though. After the shit that happened with Kamara and Ro, I decided to move in with him. I didn't feel safe at all. I made the best decision for me and my son. I knew Zoo would protect us at all costs. And I was lucky to have him. It was hard expressing my gratitude. He'd been helping a lot with Jase, taking him to and from school, cooking for him, and making sure he bathed. At times, I felt like I didn't deserve him.

"Are you good?" he asked.

He squeezed my hand to get my attention. My mind had wandered off again. I found myself doing that a lot lately.

"I'm okay," I responded.

As I walked down the aisle of the church, overwhelming pain ran through my veins. My eyes were filled with tears to the brim. The closer I got to the coffin, the harder it was to hold myself together. Zoo held onto me tightly to make it known that he had me.

Removing my black shades from my face, I looked over my friend's body in her casket. She was so beautiful laying there. I didn't think we would be able to have an open casket funeral, but she was perfect. Ms. Wade had the funeral home dress her in her favorite color, blue.

"She didn't deserve this," Ms. Wade said, walking up from behind.

It was my first time seeing her since the hospital a week ago. We'd been in contact every day, but it was too painful for me to be around people. I felt bad for not helping with the funeral arrangements, but Ms. Wade understood. She told me plenty of times that she wished she could escape all of her family and just be alone.

I hugged and held onto her as she cried into my chest. I couldn't even imagine the pain she was going through. She lost her only child. They were close, like best friends. God, we were suffering. I was ready for it all to be over with. I remember going to my parents' funeral when I was child. It was traumatizing. Funerals brought back hidden memories.

But for my best friend, I was strong. I sat through the service on the verge of breaking down the entire time, but I kept it together. I had to keep reminding myself of all the good times. Kamara was a crazy girl and didn't mind taking risks. This crazy girl had me breaking into a nigga's house and hiding under his bed. Or like the time three years ago, we got so drunk in Houston for her birthday. We got so fucked up that we ended up trying some things with each other that we never spoke of again. *Crazy.*

Zoo tapped my leg. My mind had wandered off yet again. The service was over and everyone was up and hugging each other.

"Bae, are you—"

I held my hand up to him. "I'm fine. Can we please just leave? I'm ready to go home," I said.

"Fasho. We can dip right now. But you know we still have the burial," he said.

"I just can't do this. It's too much. I'm sorry but—"

"I got you. Let me grab Ms. Wade," Zoo said.

After telling Ms. Wade we were leaving, we got on the interstate to head home. I had the urge to smoke. And I wasn't even a smoker. I just needed something to calm my nerves. I couldn't get right for shit.

"What do you think about a mini vacation?" Zoo placed his hand on my thigh as he drove. "Just somewhere for you to go alone and clear your head. And if you want, I can go with you too. Or hell, it can just be you, or you and Jase. Just tell me how to make it better," he continued.

"I don't know." I shrugged my shoulders. "I'll think about it," I said.

Bzzt. Bzzt. Bzzt. Zoo's phone vibrated and the hospital's number Bluetoothed across the car's screen. He jumped to answer the phone. I knew he was hoping to hear good news about Romeo. Hell, we all needed some kind of good news.

"Hi, is this Zachary Slaid?" An Indian accent came over the speakers.

"Yeah, what's good, Doc?"

"I was calling to inform you that Romeo woke up twenty minutes ago."

"Word? I'm on the way," Zoo responded. He hung up before even giving the doctor a chance to say anything else.

Merging over to the farthest lane on the right, we got off on the next exit that came up. For the first time, I had a little hope. I wanted to know what happened. How did my friend become a victim? I was lost. I needed answers.

But then I thought about it. "Zoo, he doesn't know about Kamara."

"Damn, bae, you right," he said.

Neither one of us was prepared to let him know. It was silent the rest of the way to the hospital. Zoo didn't even play any music. I think we both needed peace and quiet. I definitely didn't wanna hear any rap music about killings, drugs, and pussy. That was the only type of music Zoo listened to. But he was respectful enough to just keep it silent.

"You don't have to go in if it's too much for you. You can take the car home and I'll Uber home later," Zoo suggested when we pulled into the parking garage.

"Nah, I'm coming in. I gotta know why that happened to my friend."

He nodded and we headed inside. I sent Ms. Wade a text and told her that Ro was awake too. I knew she was busy with the funeral but I wanted to keep her in the loop. She deserved to know why this happened to her daughter. We needed closure.

"Uh, Mr. Slaid!" Ro's doctor called out from the nurses' station. We were just about to walk in. "Can I speak to the both of you before you go in to see him?"

"What's up, Doc?"

"There are a few things I need to discuss with you before you go see him. Romeo is paralyzed from the waist down and has little movement in his upper body right now. We presume the paralysis is temporary. With aggressive therapy, he may be able to walk again in a few weeks. His larynx is bruised and swollen from the intubation, so he won't be able to speak for a few days. Right now, he's been using a notepad to communicate. We have contacted the local police department to let them know he's awake. They have a few questions for him. A detective should be here soon to speak with him."

Zoo grabbed her by her arm and pulled her in for a hug.

"I appreciate you, Doc. I really do."

"No problem. But I also want to mention that he keeps writing the name Kamara on the notepad. I remember that Kamara Wade didn't make it. We didn't share this information with him because we didn't want to aggravate his condition if he became too upset or irrational. Romeo is at a very critical stage in his recovery. He cannot afford to back track."

"I can't lie to my mans like that," Zoo said.

"Then you risk saving his life. He has already proved to be confrontational. When we told him we couldn't give him information on another patient that's not a relative, he clenched his fists in anger and his blood pressure shot to the roof. Now is not the time to upset him even more."

Shaking his head, Zoo grabbed me by the hand and we went to Romeo's room. I didn't know if he was gonna tell him or not. I decided to just follow his lead.

"My brother, how are you feeling?" Zoo asked.

He had bandages covering him from the neck down. He looked horrible and the pain was evident. He scribbled on the notepad and slid it over to Zoo. It read *Kamara*.

"Look man, we don't have much time to do this because the cops are on the way to come and question you. I need you to tell me who's responsible for this shit."

Ro used the pen to point to Kamara's name. He ignored everything Zoo said to him. He was only worried about one thing, my friend.

Zoo sighed. "She's over in the other room, man. She's fighting for her life just like you. She's not awake yet though. But aye, I need to know who did this shit to y'all."

He sighed. I knew if he could talk he would cuss Zoo the fuck out. Scribbling just below Kamara's name, he wrote, *the Italians. Angelo's people.*

CHAPTER SIX
KAREEM "REEM" BANKS

My daddy once told me that I fuck up everything I touch. I hate that he was right. For some reason, I just couldn't get right. I didn't know if my choice to bang with a gang was smart, but it was my only route for survival. And after what happened yesterday, I knew I had to take out a guard today.

They beat my ass so bad yesterday in the mess hall that I was released from the infirmary this morning. Them niggas busted my incision back open and the doc had to sew me back up. That shit hurt like a bitch. She stitched shit without pain meds or numbing cream. I was still in pain. And I knew these niggas would not let me catch a break unless I was protected. So I was catching that body, and I already had the entire plan together.

After lying in my cell for a few more minutes, I waited for Macho to leave. *Action.* I started walking around the cell, groaning and moaning like I was in pain. That grabbed the guard's attention. I could see him eyeing me from my peripheral vision. Once my back was turned to him, I sat on the end of my bed and stuck my fingers down my throat to make myself vomit. In seconds, my sheets were covered in last night's dinner.

They already knew about me detoxing, so me throwing up wasn't out of the ordinary.

"What the fuck, inmate?" He stared at me in disgust. "I wish they would send yo' junkie ass to a medical facility already," he complained. He gagged when I wiped the remainder from my mouth with my forearm.

"I need some new sheets," I said.

"I'm not touching that shit! Wrap it up in a ball and follow me to the laundry."

Music to my ears. I followed him to the laundry room. I knew it would be empty around this time, giving me plenty of opportunity to make my move. I found a shank hidden in the bathroom two days ago and snatched it, taking it straight to my cell.

I'd been saving it for this very moment. When the door behind us closed, I threw my dirty sheets over his head, making him panic. I slid the shank from behind my back and went to work. I stabbed him over and over in the back. He fell to the floor and laid in a puddle of his blood.

The image of him lying there brought back memories of Quesha. Memories that were hard for me to stomach. I felt lightheaded, but I had to man the fuck up. I shook the thoughts out of my head and focused back on the mission at hand. I took the sheet off of his head and cleaned my vomit off of his face.

I threw my dirty sheets into the washer and grabbed a new set. I was careful to cover all of my tracks. Zoo always taught me that. I was in and out without a peep. Once I went back to my cell, I made my bed back up and laid there for a while for accountability. I wanted Macho to see me when he got back so it would look like I had an alibi. I had to play that shit as normal as possible. So for the next two hours, I stayed in my cell and carried on a minor conversation with Macho when he returned.

After I felt that I was good, I went to find Slug and the guys to let them know I came through. I had to tie a shirt around my face again so no one would notice who I was. Every time niggas saw me, they gave me a hard time. I figured out a system to outsmart their asses though. I always found ways to keep my face covered when going outside of my cell.

"You got sum fa me, lil' nigga?" Slug asked as I approached the crew. I nodded. "Man, take that shit off yo' head," he continued.

I snatched the shirt off and let it fall to the floor. "He's in the laundry room," I said.

He sent his boys to go and check it out. They returned in five minutes and told Slug I was legit. The knot in my stomach finally loosened just a little. Slug looked down at me and smirked.

"Damn, I'm proud. I didn't think you would pull it off."

"So I'm good?"

"Fasho." He placed his arm around my shoulder. "Nigga, you took out a guard, we in deep with each other now, slime."

Relief came over me. God knew I had been waiting to hear those magical words. "Bet."

"Shit is gon' get hot around here when they find this guard. So I want you to just sit still for me. When the pressure lets up, I'mma show you our drug operation around here."

"Drugs?" That shit made my mouth water.

He chuckled. "You have a lot to learn, young blood. We run this shit. Every day we get pills from the inmates that get medicine on pill call. They cheek 'em until they catch up with us."

"Word?"

"That's nothing. Like I said, we run the prison. You'll see."

CHAPTER SEVEN
SAVANNAH "VANNAH" GOOD

Back again for another session. I wished they would just leave me be. I'd told them time after time that I was happy here. Getting out was the least of my worries. But I barely had any say so over my own life here. They made all the decisions for me. I didn't have the luxury to opt out of therapy; it was mandated.

Ms. Reyes brought me in for therapy early today. She said she had something important to tell me on the way to her office. This was a first. I didn't know what to think. She liked to play mind games though. Her *important information* may just be a way to weasel information out of me. She was good at that.

"How are you doing, Savannah?" she asked. She sat across from me.

"I'm good." Yep, I had an attitude. "Can we get to the important news?" I was very impatient. I was ready to see what she had to say.

"Of course. Well, your parents hired another lawyer on your behalf and she had forensics go back through the evidence. Then new evidence was brought to the court... The person who murdered Quesha was taller than her. And you're shorter than Quesha. There was no way you were capable of causing those injuries. You told me you didn't do it, and I doubted you. I'm sorry for that," she said.

"Wh-what? Does that mean I'm free to go?"

"Not quite. You're still facing charges for Blessing... Savannah, you made a mistake. I know deep down you love your daughter. Let's make it right. Tell me what happened."

Reaching inside of her desk, she pulled out photos and slid them over to me. There were a few pictures of Maya and one picture of Blessing. It was a hospital picture. She still had her ankle monitor. She was so cute. And Maya, her smile was contagious. I caught myself smiling. I sighed.

"After the situation with Reem—"

"What situation?" she asked.

"After Reem came to my house and assaulted me in front of our daughter," I said. I was firm on that.

"Okay, go on."

"Well, if you didn't know, they took him to jail and left me with the baby. I couldn't look at her without crying. I tried to pick her up but I didn't feel right. We didn't have a connection and I didn't feel like a mother. I knew something was wrong. I knew I was ill. I wasn't in the right mind to care for my child. I needed help. So I drove to my mom's house and she wasn't there. I called her back to back but she didn't answer. That's when I decided to drive to Birmingham, Alabama. That's where my daddy lives. I called him to make sure he was home and he was there. I didn't tell him I was coming though. I just told him to stay by his phone. Everything was going well until she started crying. She cried for an hour straight with no break. I got so frustrated that I got off an exit in a city called Hoover, Alabama. There was a Subway right off the exit. I parked in their parking lot and got out to check on her. I realized that she had poop all over her and she was hungry. I felt so bad. I had nothing for her. And I don't know what brought me to do it, but I took her entire car seat into the bathroom and left her there. It was a relief. But that's the last I've seen of her."

CHAPTER EIGHT
ZACHARY "ZOO" SLAID

'Posed to be chasing money
But you chasing b!tches (What you doing?)
Real bosses don't talk
We just sit back and listen (Uhh huh!)
Stack that paper up and then make boss moves (Yeah!)
She like to argue, so I sent that b!tch to law school

Dolph blasted through the speakers of my Lambo truck while me and Chip smoked a blunt. He'd been out of the state for his mom's wedding. He didn't know anything about Romeo and Kamara until he got back today. He had been trying to get in contact with Ro too, but I couldn't bother him while he was celebrating for his OG. But the moment he touched down, I put him on game. Bro couldn't believe it either. He was ready to kill sum.

"Yo' ole lady good?" Chip asked.

I sighed. "Nah. This shit is killing her," I said.

"Damn, I don't even know what to say, man."

"Say less. All we need to do is carry out this plan. We going body for body. "

"Oh, we most definitely gon' up the sco' on these niggas. I'm ready when you are," Chip said.

We'd been sitting outside the Steakhouse the Italians owned for the last three hours. Both of the brothers were inside along with their boys. When Ro told me who was responsible, I hopped on the line ASAP and got all the information I needed. I constructed a plan and waited for Chip to get back in town. To say I was fed up was an understatement. I had no more patience. I was tired of niggas fucking with me and mine.

"Stay here. I'll be back," I said.

Stepping out of the car, I sat my gun on the seat and grabbed my knife from the dashboard. The restaurant's closed sign flashed bright red. They were closed on Sundays so no guests were inside, just the niggas I wanted to see. I walked through the front door and followed the sound of voices to the back.

I pushed the door open and every set of eyes fell to me. I didn't have time to play, so I popped it off quickly. Time was of the essence. My eyes bounced around the room to see what I was up against. There were five niggas in total.

"I'm looking for the brother of Angelo," I said.

Two niggas drew their guns and aimed them at me. "I wouldn't do that if I were you. 'Cause then we'd all die. And I didn't plan on dying today... But y'all will."

They lowered their guns and chuckled together. Two of them clanged their beers together with grins over their faces. They took me for a joke. But see, they had the wrong mutha-fucka. "Who are you? You humor us," one said.

"You went after my brother!"

"Oh, he's talking about the black kid and his girl that we shot," one of them said.

They all laughed louder together while I sat there with brewing anger. "I feel sorry for you, my friend. You came all the way here to die a miserable death just like your friend," one of them threatened.

"Yeah right. I have a question though. Who told you that my mans had anything to do with your brother's death?"

He went to laugh again but suddenly grabbed his head. He wasn't feeling too good and I knew why. "You good, boss?" one of his boys asked.

My plan was happening right on time. To speed things up, I brought up the issue again. "You were saying?"

Irritability and confusion had kicked in at that point. His mood changed from joking to sinister. "Our brother wasn't green to the streets, you dumb fuck. He knew someone was following him. All it took was a gun to his head for the driver to flip on your boy. Angelo gave him ten thousand to stay quiet about their encounter. My brother had already put us on about the obsessed neighbor. All fingers pointed to him when he showed up to his house for days and he wasn't there."

"Say less," I said.

I turned to walk away but stopped when he called out to me. "You must be a foolish man to think you're gonna walk out of here alive," he threatened while rubbing his throat.

He tried to stand but began to excessively cough, then he dropped his gun to the floor. His boys rushed over to him to make sure he was okay but soon, they started to lose balance and fell to the floor too.

"Not feeling too well, huh?"

"Wh-what...the fuck...did you do?" He struggled to breathe as he spoke.

"Careful there, gangsta." I squatted down to his level. "I told you that I wouldn't be dying today. But in case you're confused, I'll help you out."

He spit at me and it landed directly on top of my shoe, further pissing me off. But I kept my cool. "For the past three hours, carbon monoxide has been seeping through your vents at a slow but lethal pace. Firing a gun will ignite a fire, blowing us all to death. But none of you are even capable of firing a gun at this point. You couldn't lift a finger if I paid you, my nigga." I looked around and they were all clutching their throats, laid around on the floor. "You see, right before I came in, I had my boy up the dose, killing you a lot faster. I had approximately ten minutes to get in and out without being affected by the fumes. But it's a little too late for y'all. Right now, you should be dizzy, confused, and extremely weak. Your respiratory system is failing as I speak. Death will shortly follow... But I think I'll go ahead and take care of you now," I said.

I pulled his head back and slit his throat with the knife that I had tucked away. I felt somewhat accomplished. I wish I could've tortured them niggas until I drained every ounce of blood from their bodies. But there was no time for that. This shit had to be handled differently. We couldn't have a shootout in the middle of the day, that would draw cops. And those niggas rolled like wolves, always in a pack. It was too hard to get them alone. And I was too anxious. I wanted revenge and I still wasn't done. After I finished up inside, I headed back to the car.

"Blow that shit up," I told Chip.

We left the area and Chip pressed the detonator. The entire building went up in flames, we could see it from a block over. I had a thing for fires. It was my favorite strategy to get rid of any and all evidence of me being involved. And the likelihood of a nigga ever surviving a fire was slim.

"Where to now?" Chip asked.

"Take me to this muthafucking driver Ro hired. We need to see 'bout him. This nigga flipped on my boy, so it ain't shit he can say to me."

"Bet that up."

CHAPTER NINE

LENOIR HOLLIS

They weren't lying when they said beauty hurts. The worst of the pain was gone but my body was still sore. Tylenol seemed to help with that though. I'd been able to go out like normal. And when I say normal, I mean without cringing in pain in front of people.

Today was my first real outing. I came to the mall to purchase some clothes that would fit me but then I realized, I didn't know what type of clothes Zoo liked to see his woman laced in. He seemed like the type of man to want his woman to be dripped in name-brand attire but then again, I didn't know. So I did some cliché shit and stalked his girlfriend's Instagram.

The type of outfits she wore were not what I expected. Most of her pictures were taken in lounge clothes with the occasional club outfits. It wasn't nothing name brand for sure. Her clothes seem to come from Pretty Little Thing or Fashion Nova. Her style was easy to match. I revamped my whole closet to match her style, and I didn't stop there.

Sis had her hair laid in a different style on every picture. Even if it was something simple, it was cute. The box braids I always wore had to go. I pulled out my phone to go through her Instagram once more when I saw what she posted on her Instagram story. *Hair Cut Day.* The short snippet showed her at the mall with her son. It had to be a sign. I was in the mall and I just happened to be in the mall the same day and time. I just knew it was a sign.

Call me crazy, stupid, or a lunatic. I don't give a damn. I had invested too much into that man to not go all in. There was only one barbershop in the mall that all of the Black people went to, The Crossroads. So tracking her down was not hard at all. I sat in a nearby nail shop that gave me the perfect view of the barbershop. They were just walking up as I was picking out my color for the nail technician.

What surprised me most, it wasn't just her and her son. Zoo and his son were also trailing along. They looked like the perfect family. Or so I thought. I took extra notice of the fact that they didn't look so happy. They actually looked sad. I didn't know why, but it was perfect for me. I hoped things between them didn't work out so it would be easier for me to swoop in and grab my man.

I kept my eyes on them the entire time. I wanted to see how he treated her and more importantly, why he loved her the way he did. And from what I could see, he seemed to be wrapped around her finger. He took the boys into the barbershop and took out a stack of bills and handed it to her. Straight like that. He ran his fingers through her natural hair and pointed to the hair salon next door.

I rolled my eyes in jealousy and focused my attention back to the nail polishes. I chose a light pink color and handed it to the technician. All while she did my nails, my thoughts were only of Zoo and Zaryah. I knew for a fact in order to pull that man, I was gon' have to one up his lil' girlfriend. He was in love-love. I could tell by the way he looked at her.

He already said the pussy was good, so that was a plus for me. And he hit my shit with a condom on. If he fucked raw, I knew I'd have a hold on him then. There was one problem, though, the nigga wanted to be *business partners* instead of fucking with me on another level.

"That color is so cute," the lady next to me complimented.

"Right. I was thinking about adding some rhinestones," I said.

"You definitely should. It would be cute," she said.

I smiled. And from there, we carried on small talk while we got manicures and pedicures. She was a talker. I sat there and listened to her tell me her whole life story. It was actually kinda interesting too. Her social life was a lot more exciting than mine, that was for sure.

"Why do you keep looking over there at the hair salon?" she asked.

"Just trying to figure out if I really wanna get my hair done today."

"Oh really? You should let me do your hair one day. I start working at that shop in two weeks. I came by to drop off some of my products in my booth over there, but I saw someone inside that doesn't really fuck with me. So I'mma wait for her to leave, then I'mma go."

"Girl, what? You sound scared. One of those bitches in there got you shook like this?"

"Tuh, girl. Sometimes you learn from your fuck ups. I don't want any more bad dealings with those people," she said.

"What people?" I looked over to the salon.

"Zoo and his girl. I used to work in his salon but some shit went down and one of the owner's girlfriends beat my ass and then they fired me." She paused for a minute and looked down at her nails. "But they had every right to, so I ain't trippin'. I'm just tryna move on," she said.

What the fuck? She had my entire attention then. "What did you tell me your name was again?"

"Asia."

"Oh yeah. That's pretty."

"Thank you." She glanced back over to the salon. "Although we had our differences, I feel bad for them. It's sad what happened to their friends."

"Huh? What friends? What are you talking about?"

"They got shot up. Kamara Wade died a little while ago. And last I heard, Romeo's still in the hospital. It's been all over the news and social media," she said.

As she talked, a master plan brewed in my head. She seemed to know a lot about that crew and I could use an ally. Hell, I could just use a friend. I had no one to vent to about my frustrations. I had to pace myself though. Asia was terrified of them. That ass whooping had to be severe.

"Wow, I didn't know any of that... You know, you're a cool person and I like you. You can definitely do my hair anytime, girl."

"Bet. Here, lock your number in my phone," she said. She handed her phone over to me and I saved my number under Lenoir with the nails emoji.

We spent the rest of the manicure talking about any and everything. She caught on to me when she noticed I kept steering the conversation back to the topic of Zoo.

"Am I missing something? Because you keep mentioning Zoo for some reason."

"Guilty," I said with a cute smile. "There is a reason. We kinda been fucking around," I continued.

"So you're his side piece?"

"No, I mean, yeah. But not for long," I said.

She stood up. "Wait, so you came here to spy on them?! That's wild. And I don't know what it is that you think, but that man is not letting up on Zaryah Cox. He will never be yo' man, sis." She looked over at the salon one last time. "You know what, I actually won't be able to do yo' hair. Any dealings with them is dangerous. And I advise you to leave it alone before you find yourself hurt or dead," she warned.

She asked her technician to move her to another seat so she could get far away from me. Talking to her sent chills through me. That ended quickly. But despite what she said, I still walked my happy ass over to the salon when she left and got the same exact style as Zaryah Cox.

CHAPTER TEN

ZARYAH "RYAH" COX

I thought about what Zoo said and took him up on his offer about a 'mommy and me' trip. The amount of stress I was under was too hectic. Since Jase had school, I was only able to do a weekend trip, which was fine with me. If I could get away for a day, I would've been grateful. I needed a break from Atlanta.

I was cool with just going on a mini vacation to somewhere like the mountains or somewhere. But Zoo being Zoo had to go all out. He booked us a weekend trip in Puerto Rico. I didn't even fuss with him. I took the itinerary and packed me and my son's bags. Zoo wanted to come along, but I honestly needed a break from him too. I told him to hold off on that. He had to stay behind.

He'd been hiding something from me and I honestly didn't have the energy to even bitch and try to figure out what it was. His energy had been different for a hot lil' minute, but I was trying to give him time to tell me what was going on. And this energy was before we found out about Ro and Kamara. But everything that's done in the dark comes to the light.

"I'm ready, Mommy," Jase said to me.

He had his shirt on inside out and toothpaste was on the side of his mouth but he was the cutest. He even had his tiny Paw Patrol backpack on. Grabbing him by his hand, I helped him get himself together before we left the house. I couldn't have my boy half stepping.

"What do you have inside of this backpack?" I asked.

"I have my stuff that you told me to pack," he said. His voice was so cute and innocent. "I packed my tablet, my crayons, and TiTi Mara's coloring book," he continued.

He caught me off guard with his last statement. "What'd you say?"

I grabbed his backpack and searched the insides as he explained to me what he was talking about. I pulled out a tablet, a charger, some crayons, and a notebook with a lock. *A diary?* "Where'd you get this from?" I asked, holding it up so he could see.

"I got it from TiTi's house at the cookout," he said.

He meant funeral. Anytime we ever went around any type of large gathering of close friends or family, he always called it a cookout.

"I'll hold onto this, baby. This isn't a coloring book," I said.

I tucked it down into my carry-on bag for the plane. I was curious as to why Mara's overgrown ass had a diary. I smiled at the thought. She was so unpredictable. Grabbing my attention, Zoo came downstairs with the keys in his hand.

"Y'all ready, bae?" he asked.

"Yeah, I just gotta take the bags to the car," I said.

"Bruh, quit playing with me like I'm really about to let you take these bags to the car," he fussed. He shook his head from side to side. "Go and get in the car. Let the men handle this," he continued. He pointed between him and Jase.

I loved how he was with Jase. Zoo was a natural. He always

included Jase in everything he did. It was like he was teaching him how to be a little man. Kareem never did any of that shit. The most he would do was watch him when I needed him to, and he would throw a basketball around the house with Jase, no real bonding. Zoo actually took up time with Jase and learned about him. He did the same with Hendrix too. I was proud of the man he was becoming.

He was perfect besides whatever he was hiding from me. We had so much against us that we couldn't win. But I was willing to keep working at our relationship. I knew he loved me and I loved him. But in order for us to continue to work, I felt like I had to find some peace. This trip was about me and my son. I had big plans for us to disconnect from the universe and bond together.

"You're so fucking beautiful," Zoo complimented. He used the back of his hand to brush my cheek. "And I see the look in your eyes. It's gon' get better. I promise," he continued.

I placed my hand on top of his and smiled. No words would come out but a smile was enough. We buckled up and got on the interstate toward the airport. The traffic was heavy and I ended up dozing off until we arrived.

* * *

THE AIRPORT

We finally made it to our destination, and I pulled my arms above my head for a much-needed stretch. One of the worst things about Atlanta was the traffic, and that delayed us big time. I was worried about missing the flight the few times I would peep up from my nap but Zoo told me to keep sleeping, he had it taken care of.

"You okay love?" he asked, licking his lips.

"Yeah, I'm fine. I'm just confused," I said. I stepped out of the car and looked around. "I've never been on an airplane before, but I thought there would be a lot more people and planes," I continued.

I looked around to take in the scenery once more. We were the only people there.

"Really, Ryah? You know damn well I'm not letting you ride through an airline when *we* have all this money. I booked y'all a private plane."

Smiling, I walked over to him and kissed him on the lips. "Thank you, baby."

"Fasho. But look, are we good? We vibing?" He pointed between us. The look in his eyes was concerning. He knew our balance had been thrown off. He felt that shit just like I felt it. I used that moment to ask a question I'd had on the tip of my tongue for some time.

"Have you ever thought about getting out of the streets, Zoo? I mean really getting out. With the amount of money you have, you could do anything you want. Why do you love that lifestyle so much?"

He was so stunned he couldn't speak. He didn't expect me to throw this at him. He looked away and licked his lips. "Please don't leave me, Zaryah."

"I can tell when a man is hiding something from me, Zoo."

I stared at him momentarily then walked away to get my son. I knew what happened to Kamara wasn't Zoo's fault, but I realized something. Zoo's street affiliations would always put me and my son at risk. Of what, I didn't know. But I didn't wanna risk Jase being killed because of some type of street shit.

I wouldn't leave Zoo without giving him the opportunity to do better though. That's why I brought up the subject about him getting out of the streets. He had a son to think about as well, which should've made the decision much easier. He needed to know that all money earned didn't have to be dirty. It was up to him to do what was right though. I stood on what I said.

"Ryah, can we talk a little more about this shit before you leave?"

"Zoo, listen, I'm not mad at all. I'm exhausted. You have been nothing but good to me. I love being with you. It's the lifestyle that's scaring me. I'm not leaving you, but I want you to take some deep consideration into what I just said before it gets to that point," I said.

"I got you."

We shared a long hug then we parted ways. The pilot took our luggage and loaded it onto the back of the plane as the stewardess guided us aboard.

"Hi, my name is Susie and I'll be your flight attendant. You guys can make yourselves comfy anywhere in the general area. Let me know if you need anything and I'll be happy to help. We should arrive in three hours and thirty minutes," she said.

"Great," I smiled.

Jase and I took a seat in the middle of the plane. I was still a little tired so I laid my seat all the way back. It was like a mini-bed with a tiny pillow for comfort. Jase, on the other hand, waited right for me to get comfortable to call my name. I can't count the number of times I hear mommy in a day. Sitting up, I saw that he needed help with charging his iPad. Zoo had just gotten him that thing and he could never keep it charged.

It was as dead as a doorknob. I reached into his backpack and grabbed his iPad and charger. I found a space under the seat for a plug. And to keep him from bothering me anymore, I reached into my carry-on to give him some snacks. That's when I saw Kamara's diary sticking out the side. I looked at the front of it and smiled. I still couldn't believe her overgrown ass had a diary. It kinda felt like an invasion of privacy, but I missed my fucking friend and wanted to hear her voice again.

After I got Jase settled, I used the back of my earring to maneuver the lock open. It took some finessing but I was able to get it. I took a deep breath and opened it to the first page. It took me a little over an hour to finish the entire thing. She mostly talked about her goals, insecurities, and random situations. Then there was one particular page that stuck out to me most. It was the last one written. It was written a few days after our argument.

Dear Diary, why is life so hard? Whoever came up with the saying, 'you can't have your cake and eat it too' told no lies. My man is the muthafucking goat when it comes to this relationship shit. The sad truth is, I'm part of the problem. Ro admitted that he has a problem with the sex and I get it. I love Ro to death, I swear, but I love Ryah more. I'm in love with my best friend and she doesn't even know it. I hate that I'm not being honest with Ro, but I could never tell him my true feelings. Ryah either.

Me and Ryah ended up getting drunk a few years ago and did some things that we never did before and I loved it. We never spoke on it again but I think about it all the time. But I know that's a line that me and Ryah would never be able to cross. I don't even know how she would take it if I told her that I was in love with her.

I know one thing for sure, I've never been so glad that she let go of that piece of shit, Kareem. If he was on fire, I wouldn't use my spit to put him out. Fuck that bum ass nigga. I don't even wanna touch on that subject 'cause that nigga ain't even worth the ink from my pen.

Now Zoo, that's a subject I wanna touch on. I like Zoo but I can't stand him at the same damn time. I can't front like he's not good to my girl. He's a good man to her but I hate that he's stealing her away from me. I still stand on everything I said about him to Ryah 'cause the nigga is dangerous as fuck but hell, I didn't even know my own nigga was in the streets, so there's that.

Diary, I just wish that I could be in a relationship with Ryah and Ro and we both live one big happy life. Is that too fucking much to ask?

I must've read that page one hundred times. I always knew Kamara had a little crush on me deep down, but I never knew she felt this deeply about me. I always thought me and her had an understanding that we only fucked around because I was mad at Kareem, we were drunk, and I just needed a scapegoat.

Had I known she had true feelings for me, we could have talked about everything. I never wanted her to feel like we couldn't talk about her feelings. Although I didn't feel the same way, I wish she would've shared her feelings with me.

I had enough of reading. I packed the diary back into my bag. I laid my seat back into a bed and the stewardess brought me a warm blanket. And I was out like a light.

CHAPTER ELEVEN

KAREEM "REEM" BANKS

"Ahh," I cried out from the bootleg tattoo being carved into my skin. This nigga had sumo-wrestler hands. The further he got along, the more it hurt. I swear it felt like he was tattooing my fucking flesh.

"Nigga, be still and quit crying like a bitch," Slug roared.

His voice sent chills down my spine. That nigga could tell me to do anything and I would do it because I was just that afraid of him. It was because of him that I was sitting here getting a tattoo to represent Bloods.

The pain was well worth it though. I knew niggas wouldn't fuck with me if they saw that I was fucking with the Bloods. That's why I was sure to get it on my arm where niggas could see it. I had a plan to never be fucked with again, and it was working out for me.

"How does it feel to be Blood?" Slug asked.

"Shit feels good. Y'all my brothers now."

"And I hope you understand the definition of Blood Brotherhood. Don't fall victim to the gang," he warned.

I nodded and swallowed spit. "I got you."

"Fasho, I know you do. That's why I gotta look out," he said. He tossed me an old beat-up flip phone and a pack of cigarettes. "That's yours. Don't get caught slipping," he continued.

"Damn, I appreciate it, Slug."

I was never expecting anything from them besides protection. Bro was putting me on fasho and I was feeling it. It was so hard to get a phone call in this bitch without money. My family had completely cut me off, so I was in this shit alone. They didn't even give a fuck about me enough to put money on my books for commissary. I bet my pops was behind that. He probably told my mama to let me man up and figure it out. Well, I had news for him, I had been figuring it out.

"Don't get caught with that shit. And only smoke those cigs in the shower with the water running so the guards won't smell the aroma."

"Bet. Aye, can I make a few calls on this bitch tho'?"

"Nigga, duh. Why the fuck else would I give it to you?" he snapped.

"Bet. I'mma catch up with y'all in a bit," I said before walking back to my cell.

It felt good to be able to walk around without having to cover up my face in fear. Now niggas knew I was repping with Bloods so they didn't want smoke. I wish I had thought of this on day one. It would've saved me a few ass whoopings.

Finally making it to my cell, I was eager to use that phone. Macho was nowhere in sight. That was good. I didn't need him in my business, with his nosey ass. It was like he wanted niggas to kill me. I didn't know how to feel about Macho. But anyways, I laid in my bunk with the cover over my head so no one could see when I made a call.

The first number I dialed was my mama, and she was on some straight bullshit.

"Hello."

"Ma—"

"Kareem? Look, Kareem, if you're calling me to beg for something, you can hang it up! It's time for you to man up, son. Whatever you need, figure it out."

The line went dead. Without a word more to say, she hung up right in my face. I knew it was coming. Those sounded like my pops' words. I knew for sure I wasn't getting any help from them. Shit hurt to know my family would turn their backs on me in my time of need. I laid there thinking about what my mama said.

That's when I realized I was getting everything that was owed to me. The same way I dogged Ryah when she went to prison for me, I was feeling her same pain times a hunnid.

I had the urge to call Ryah, but I knew I had no right. I had no right to disturb her peace with my bullshit. And as selfish as it may sound, even though I knew I would never have her again, I just felt like I needed someone. Even if it was just a frenemy. Forty-one years was a long time to count down alone. I wanted to make shit right. So I made the call anyway, going against my inner thoughts.

Ring. Ring. Ring. "Hello." Her sweet but hood voice flowed through the line.

"Hey, Ry."

"Kareem? What the fuck? How are you even calling me right now?"

Typical Ryah, she had a million questions. "I know right."

"Kar—"

"Please don't hang up, Ryah. There's something I need to say to you," I said.

She sighed into the phone. "Let me guess. You're sorry, blah blah blah. You gon' make shit right, blah blah blah. The same tired ass shit, right?"

"That's some of it. But I was also gon' say that you were always right, about everything. I was the problem, never you. And I'm not asking for anything, not even forgiveness. But since I've been in here, I understand the torture I put you through when I turned my back on you. I didn't deserve you, Zaryah, and I apologize from the bottom of my heart. And I know some of those wounds may still be fresh, so please forgive me if this is too soon, but I would love to see my son," I said.

"Kamara's dead," she said. She came straight out with it, ignoring everything I said. Which I was cool with. I was glad to get it off my chest. But I was more glad that she decided to share something with me.

"Damn, Ry. I'm so sorry that happened."

"I'm sorry, I shouldn't have—"

"No, no, no, you told me for a reason, Ryah. You haven't had a chance to vent. Kamara was always that listening ear. I know these things about you, Ryah. Don't forget that. I don't want to be your enemy forever, and I'm here to listen to whatever you have to say."

"I don't know how I got to this point in my life, but I am so disappointed in myself. If I could go back in time, I would change a lot of shit. I can't believe every time I feel like I've found myself, I lose control."

"And that's all on me, Ryah. We both could've been so much further in life if I would've gotten my shit together. But I fucked up and it's too late for me. But you and Jase still have your lives to live. A few hiccups in the road doesn't mean the world is over. Your happiness is based on you. Don't let a fuck nigga like me ever take your happiness away again. I'll say it a million times; Zaryah Cox, I'm sorry."

She chuckled. It was that very laugh that made me smile.

"And when did you become so wise? Who knew my baby daddy could have some sense?"

"I know right. I wish I would've had it when I was with you." I peeked from the covers to make sure no one was near. "But listen, I gotta go before these niggas catch me. I'm sorry about Kamara. And you can always text me at this number too. And think about what I said about Jase. Love you."

She cleared her throat. "I uh... I'll think about it," she stumbled.

Click. I wasn't looking for her to say I love you back. I was just expressing my emotions to her. I knew my chances with Ryah were over. She would never look back and I couldn't blame her for that. I fucked up, so I was accepting my losses.

That's why I hit up Geo by text and asked him to have some lil' hoes come by and see me or at least write to me. It was a stretch though. 'Cause no bitch I knew in her right mind would hold a nigga down for forty-one years.

And if I was being honest, I wouldn't even care what shorty was doing on the outside. I'd be a fool to believe a woman would keep her pussy closed until I was released. I only wanted the company. Just to have somebody to write or see from time to time would make the time much easier to bear.

I was getting ready to ask him to put money on my books when I heard hard footsteps approaching. Those were the footsteps of a guard, they liked to make their presence known. I sent Geo a text asking him if he knew any information on my daughter. And I added the message about the money for my books too. Quickly, I hid the pack of cigarettes and flip phone in a hole under the toilet. It was the same place I hid my shank. The prison was so old, it needed major work done. Our toilet had an entire hole under it and no one knew but me and Macho.

He stopped right at my cell and tapped on the bars with his baton. "Top wants to see you, fish," he growled.

That statement dropped my stomach to my ass. Any time a guard referred to the warden, they called him Top. As long as I'd been here, the warden had never asked to see me. It didn't take a rocket scientist to figure out he wanted to see me about the recent dead guard.

The CO escorted me to the warden's office, and I was surprised when I saw a familiar face. Slug sat slumped in his chair in front of the warden. Top stared at me with an evil glare and my eyes bounced from him to Slug. I was trying to read the room.

"Have a seat, Banks," Top demanded.

Dropping my head, I did as he asked. I sat my dumb ass next to Slug and prepared myself for the worst. This time around, I knew to keep my fucking mouth closed no matter what this police ass nigga threw at me.

"Do you know why y'all are here?" he asked.

Slug didn't say shit and neither did I. I learned my lesson from the last time. I didn't know shit. He started yelling and a bunch of other shit, like knocking papers off of the desk and slamming his fists down. I just held my head down and tuned his ass out with thoughts of my kids. After being charged with the rest of my life here, a new me developed. A better me, I should say.

"BANKS!" He clapped his hands in my face. "Why the fuck do I have a dead CO in the laundry room and you were the last person seen going in with him?"

I shrugged. That made him even more angry. He got in my face, mushing my head while spit flung from his lips as he spoke. I could literally smell the sausage on his breath from breakfast. He sternly looked over at Slug.

"Leave," he growled.

He picked himself up and walked outside the door where a guard was waiting for him. That left just me and Top. He sat on the end of his desk like a rhino, and I was his prey. But see, he really had me fucked up. I was no longer the bitch-ass nigga that was afraid of consequences. I felt like I had nothing left to lose inside of those prison walls, so snitching was beyond me. I wasn't going out sad again.

"Did that muthafucka force you into killing one of my guys? If he did, you can tell me and I'll personally take care of him. You ain't the first young cat he's got to do his dirty bidding. You can tell me what happened, son."

I shrugged again and before I knew it, his hand was around my neck. "I see how you wanna play! You just caught yourself another life sentence. When the feds get a load of this, they are gonna fry yo' ass until there is nothing left of you but that dirty dick of yours."

I frowned up my face. "Aye man, don't ever mention my dick. And do what you gotta do. I don't even know what you're talking about," I lied.

"So you're willing to risk adding more years to your sentence for a muthafucka you've known all of three weeks?"

"Yo, can I leave? I don't wanna miss lunch. It's cornbread day."

"Not quite, I have a few more questions for you," he said.

He came with questions all from the woodworks, trying to intimidate and scare me into telling on myself or Slug. I held my own though. He didn't hear a word from me.

CHAPTER TWELVE
ZACHARY "ZOO" SLAID

Today was already going fucked up. The hospital called me in the middle of my workout. This nigga Ro don' got his ass kicked out of the hospital. The doctor said a new nurse accidentally told him about Kamara and shit went left. He only had full mobility in his upper body, but that was all it took.

He fucked up every piece of equipment he could get his hands on. They immediately sedated him and asked me to come and get him in two days. Doc said that most of his injuries were healing fine and he should rest at home while he was grieving. In other words, 'come get this crazy muthafucker out of my hospital. His ass can heal at home.'

But damn, I was not ready for the conversation I knew was coming. He'll never forgive me for keeping that shit from him, but I knew I did what was best. Ro was a hothead, a cannon ready to burst. He would probably be dead if I had told him from the jump.

Ring! Ring! Ring! My alarm went off, alerting me that I was done with my work out. I barely worked anything out though. I couldn't focus for shit. I was losing my girl, and what she was asking me to do wasn't as easy as she thought. Niggas can't just put in a two weeks' notice and think it's all gravy. It's more to it than that. A nigga can't step down and leave the throne to anybody.

Ring! Ring! Ring! The alarm sounded off again 'cause my lazy ass never got up to stop it. I walked over to stop the alarm and saw that I had two missed calls from Sharonda and a message from Skyler saying call me. Shit with Sky still had been strained. She was still tripping about Hero and shit. It didn't make sense for her crazy ass to let me be in only one of my son's lives. She was pressed for no fucking reason. It didn't matter if a nigga providing or not, baby mama gon' find something to be mad about.

Scrolling to her contact, I called her phone. It barely rang good before she answered. "Zoo?"

"Y'all good? What's up?"

I could hear her sigh through the phone. "Look, Hendrix is out of hand, Zoo. I thought that now since you were around things would be different. His school just called me and told me that he was suspended for fighting and cursing," she said.

"The fuck?"

"Yeah. Can you go and get him and have a talk with him?"

"Have a talk with him? I'm 'bout to beat his ass if he doesn't have a good enough reason to be fighting," I threatened. As I talked on the phone, I walked to my car to go and pick up Hendrix.

"That shit don't work. I have whooped his ass before," she said.

"I got it. You probably don't be on his ass hard enough. But aye, how's Hero doing?"

"Why, Zoo?"

"What you mean why? I don't get you, Sky! One minute

you hollering about how I wasn't physically there for Hendrix and now you keeping me from my other son. What sense does that make?"

"I'm keeping him from you for a lot of reasons. One is because you're only requesting the DNA test because you're hoping that he's not your son. You're only thinking about her and her feelings in all of this, not my son! I would never lie and put a baby off on you. Hero is your fucking son, Zoo!"

"I hear you, Sky, but I need you to hear me out. Hero is four. That's so many years ago, ya feel me? I just wanna be sure that he is my son so I can be a part of his life too. My personal shit with Ryah has nothing to do with you. Quit mentioning her, Sky. That's childish."

"Uhm huh. Handle the situation with Hendrix please. I gotta go."

Click.

Baby mama was tripping big time. We didn't have a good co-parent relationship at all. We couldn't meet in the middle for shit. It's like she just wanted me to take her word that Hero was my kid. Nah, I couldn't do it. She and Ryah were lowkey the same though. They both wanted me to get out of the streets. Skyler said I should've chosen my son instead of the streets. And Ryah said that I needed to choose living over the streets. They were both right. The streets were burying me deeper and deeper as the days passed.

Ring. Ring. Ring. Sharonda. *Decline. Fuck she keep calling me for?* I turned my phone over and parked in the school's designated visitor's section. Hendrix had me on another level of hot. I was itching to get to him. And imagine my face when his teacher told me he was the aggressor. She said my mans had been bullying the other kids out of their ice-cream money for weeks. They didn't find out until one of the other kids finally got balls and punched Hendrix right in his shit.

And it didn't end there. Apparently, they got into a fight but when the teacher broke them up, Hendrix screamed all types of shit. 'Fuck you, nigga, I'mma kill you the next time I see you' was my all-time favorite. I told the teacher I would handle him. I had something for his lil' ass. I turnt up on him as soon as we got in the car.

"Fuck is yo' problem, lil' boy?"

This lil' ass muthafucka looked me dead in the eyes and said, "I'm you."

"Me? Nah, I'd never do some pussy shit like that. And one thing I won't tolerate is a fucking bully. Then you tryna act hard like you gon' do sum. Boy, you are all of seven years old," I fussed.

His next move shocked me the most. He opened up his book bag and pulled out a gun. And it was my gun at that. I reached over and snatched it from his hand.

"Hendrix, what the fuck? Have you lost yo' fucking mind?!" I slammed on brakes. "Anybody could've gotten hurt behind this shit! Hell nah, see, you don' took this shit too far! I should beat the fuck outta you, but I'mma handle yo' ass! I promise. You wanna be street so muthafucking bad, I'mma show you the streets. You ain't have no daddy before but you got one now, nigga. Shit gon' change," I growled.

I put the car back in motion. He sat there quietly the rest of the ride. I was too mad to even say shit else. I took his ass straight to the Zones and met up with Chip. He wanted to be street, I was gon' show him the streets for real.

"Get out," I ordered.

He smacked his teeth and before I knew it, I had his lil' ass jacked up by the rim of his shirt. The fear in his eyes told me I had his attention. "Fuck with me. I dare you. I will dog walk yo' ass all up and through the hood."

He nodded and I released my grip. "Get yo' ass out the car," I spat.

As he got out of the car, I pulled Chip to the side and gave him a rundown of what was going on. I needed him to scare the streets out of his lil' ass. I had plans on staying too, but Sharonda was still blowing up my phone and since I hadn't heard from her in almost a year, I figured it had to be important.

"You already know I got you, bro. I know you got a lot of shit you're dealing with. I got this handled for you. I'll drop him off later on tonight," he said.

I hopped in my car without another word, and Hendrix looked around like I was crazy.

"Daddy! Daddy!" he called for me.

"Nigga, I know you ain't calling for yo' daddy in the hood," Chip said with a chuckle.

"Where am I? I wanna leave," he said.

"Nah, you good. You in the streets, my boy. Yo' silver spoon ass think it's cool to disrespect yo' mama and give ya teachers a hard time, right? You wanna be in the streets, right? Let's get it," Chip responded.

I gave a salute to Chip then I drove off.

* * *

One thing about my family, they were selfish. Everybody but my OG, of course. I was in the hospital not too long ago and Sharonda didn't even think to come and check on me. Hell, a call would've been aite, but she didn't even do that. But I guess I could blame the drugs for that. She was back on that shit.

I never admitted to anyone, but my OG was right when she said me and Sharonda were just alike. I realized that over the past few weeks. When I was younger, I would always wonder, *what type of mother can't give up drugs for their kid?* And here I was, couldn't get out of the streets for mine. We were more alike than I thought, and I hated it. I didn't want any ties with her, but it was always hard to turn the other way when your supposed mother calls.

I wanted to be a cold ass nigga and turn my back to her, but I couldn't. She ended up sending me a text saying it was an emergency. The follow-up message had the address to where she was. It led me to an old abandoned house in the projects in Decatur.

It was run down too. Every single window was boarded up except for one. The window next to the door had shredded curtains dangling. Cobwebs draped over the open doorway. There was even a stench of rotten eggs flowing from somewhere.

I tucked my gun and walked through the front door. The scent got stronger when I went inside. I screwed my face up and looked around. The walls were peeling, the ceiling was caving in, and random junk was thrown everywhere.

"Sharonda!" I called out.

She came around the corner slowly, holding her head down. She looked a damn mess. She had on an oversized hoodie and pants that swallowed her tiny frame. The stench of crack was all over her. I shook my head.

The drugs were eating her ass alive. Her hair was thinning and she was hella skinnier than what I could remember.

"Why you keep calling me, man?"

"I have a problem, son," she said. Her mouth was twisted to the side when she talked and her speech was slurred.

"Don't call me that. You call me Zoo, nothing else," I snapped. "Now what problem do you have? I need to handle something with my son," I continued.

"Son? You have a kid, Zoo? I'm a grandma?" She tried to act concerned.

"Again, what problem do you have?"

She told me to follow her, and she led me to the back of the house. Sharonda had always been on drugs, but this was the worst I had ever seen her. Her skin was covered in sores and her teeth were rotten. It brought tears to my eyes to even see her like that.

"Right there," she pointed.

I looked over to the corner and there was a young girl curled up in a ball. She had stab wounds all over her.

"What the fuck?" I rushed over to see if she was alive. "Sharonda, what the fuck is going on? Whose kid is this?" I asked.

"S-s-she's no kid. She's eighteen."

I hopped to my feet and stepped to her. "Like I said, whose fucking kid is this and what happened to her? Because she's dead!"

"Z-Z-Zoo." She could barely keep focus. She looked everywhere but at me.

I threw my head back in frustration. Her ass needed a fix. She was feening. Her hands were shaking like a stripper and she could barely function. I tried to hold it back, but I couldn't. A tear rolled down my face. It broke me down to see her in that state. And in all of my life, I never tried to get her any help. I just continued to blame her for everything. At least Ro put his moms in a home. I just put mine in the back of my head like she wasn't shit to me.

"Sharonda, I need you to focus and tell me what happened to this little girl. Did you do this shit?"

"I-I-I found h-h-her texting my b-boyfriend."

"Boyfriend? Yo' what?"

"She was texting my boyfriend, Earl Mathis. A-and—"

"And so you fucking killed her? Then you talking about coke-head Earl Mathis like that nigga ain't a whole pedophile out here. He's known for preying on them high school girls!"

I grabbed my head in disbelief. "So what you want me to do? Clean up yo' shit, huh? Y'all don't give a fuck about me but as soon as y'all need sum, y'all call me."

"Zoo, I'm pregnant. That's why I did it."

"Wh-what, Sharonda?"

She held up her shirt and true enough, she had a baby pudge. And she was very pregnant. I stared at her long and hard. I wanted to slap the rest of her fucking teeth that she had in her mouth, on the ground. She had no right to be sitting up here pregnant.

I swallowed hard. "What the fuck are you doing, bruh? You forty-three fucking years old, cracked out, and talking about a baby. You don't even have an address for real."

"Can you help me or not, Zoo?"

"Heh, I'mma help yo' ass alright. I'm taking yo' ass straight to the abortion clinic."

"I'm not—"

"You're not putting another baby through that pain! I refuse!"

I snatched her up and made her get in the car. I didn't have time to deal with a body, so I had to let my young niggas handle it while I took her ass to the nearest abortion clinic. Siri sent me to one twenty minutes away. The whole ride she kept telling me how she was gon' do better with this kid and blah blah blah. Whole time, she was feening for a hit and rambling off anything.

I felt bad for dragging her down there, but I had no choice. Even if the baby was still alive, it would probably have every chromosome abnormality because of her drug use. Her body didn't even look healthy enough to carry a child. She looked like she hadn't eaten in weeks and her legs were like toothpicks. She was hanging on by a thread.

"Get out," I said when we arrived.

I had already warned her not to say shit when we got inside. She had a seat far away from everybody else while I went to talk to the lady at the front desk. They tried to hit me with 'you have to have an appointment.' But I shut that down fast when I dropped two wads of hundreds behind the counter. It was about ten G's. The doctor brought us back before anyone else.

He squeezed the clear gel on her belly and started looking for the baby. Shit was embarrassing. She was up in there looking like something off of the streets. Her face was all sunken in, clothes were dirty, and what was left of her hair was matted together. I had gotten used to the smell but I could see the staff was just warming up to it. I could tell from how they would crinkle up their noses in disgust and peel away from her. They ended up putting on masks.

"Well, I'm sorry, sir, but it looks like she is too far along to perform an abortion. She's twenty-five weeks pregnant...with twins," he said.

CHAPTER THIRTEEN
ROMEO "RO" WALTON
HOSPITAL

"Alright, Mr. Walton, all of your medications and paperwork is in this bag here. Don't forget that you have physical therapy three times a week for the next two months. Your friend is outside the door waiting for you," the nurse said.

I snatched the bag from her hands and let out a sigh. They had my limp ass posted up in a wheelchair. I didn't have much movement in my legs but I had little feeling. I was a miserable soul. I felt like I couldn't do shit for myself. The nurse even had to roll me outside because I didn't have enough strength in my arms to roll myself.

When I came face to face with Zoo, I didn't have much to say to him. I hadn't talked to him since he told me that he took care of the Italians. That was all I needed to know. It didn't bother me at all that I was shot. I knew what came with the game. But it fucked me up when they told me that Kamara died two weeks ago. And if I remember correctly, Zoo had just told me she was alive and fighting for her life.

Unbelievable. When they told me Kamara was dead, something just came over me and I spazzed out. The love of my fucking life was gone. She was murdered, all because of me.

Ms. Wade came by to see me during my stay. She told me they had Kamara's funeral and everything. Shit broke me down. She asked me how I was doing and how I was feeling. Then came the very question I knew was coming, 'what happened, Romeo?' She wanted to hear it from me even though I knew Ryah had already told her.

I told her the truth. I told her that Kamara was murdered because of me. She turnt up on me too. She jumped on my ass and called me every name she could think of. She was hurt, so I couldn't even be mad. After she calmed down, we ended up crying together. I was glad she could forgive me because Ryah couldn't. I overheard her in the room, telling Zoo that she never wanted to see me again. We were all mad at each other for some reason.

Ms. Wade told me not to be mad with Zoo for not telling me about Kamara though. She explained to me why the doctor asked him to do it. I was still lowkey pissed, but I knew he had a good reason. I just wasn't ready to deal with that shit.

We stayed quiet the entire wheelchair ride to the car but the minute we got inside, he started with the talking. "I already went by your place and got some clothes for you. You can stay at my place while you're recovering. That way we can help you out," he said.

"I appreciate it, but I'm good."

"I can't take you back to that house, man," he said.

"Man, fuck that house. I'm not going there either. Take me to the Ritz Carlton and I'll get a suite," I said.

"And who's supposed to help you, Ro? The doctor said—"

"Nigga, fuck that. I don't give a fuck what no bitch-ass doctor say," I interrupted. "Plus, I know how Zaryah feels about me. I'm not going anywhere that I'm not welcomed. I'm straight," I continued.

"You straight but you still in a wheelchair? I can handle Ryah. You need—"

"Bruh, just chill. I told you what I wanted."

"Aite, I'll let you have your attitude because I know you're going through some shit. And I'll take you to the Ritz. But I'm still gon' be checking up on you whether or not we have our differences right now."

"We ain't got no differences, man. I know why you did what you did and I ain't tripping. I'm just not interested in everybody walking on eggshells around me and babying me. I just want my time alone so I can process this shit. And I don't need you on my nuts to do that," I said.

He nodded. "I can understand that," he said.

He took me to the Ritz like I asked and what I thought was gon' be simple, was not. Zoo got my wheelchair out the trunk of the car but I had absolutely no movement in my legs yet, so he had to pick my big ass up and put me in the chair. Shit was embarrassing. People were walking by, staring and shit.

Then we finally got up to the suite and I couldn't even move myself from my chair to the bed.

"You sure you don't wanna come back to my place? We got you, man. You know it ain't even like that with us," Zoo suggested.

"I'm good!" I snapped. "If I need some extra help, I'll hire a nurse. Can you please fucking leave, bruh," I continued.

"Aite, say less."

Finally, alone.

CHAPTER FOURTEEN

ZARYAH "RYAH" COX
BACK FROM VACATION

T hat vacation was everything I felt I needed. I ended up extending it for two days because we were enjoying it just that much. I was able to clear my head and come to the realization that my friend was forever gone. I broke down a few times but it was needed. I cried and screamed it out. And my little man needed the vacation just as much as me. We bonded and talked about everything that was bothering him.

He talked to me about his daddy, and I never knew he felt the way he did. He had a strong dislike for Kareem. Reem would have to wait on that visitation because Jase wasn't going for it. He loved his daddy, sure enough, but he couldn't forget the pain that Reem put us through. But we talked through all of his problems because I wanted him to know that his feelings were important too.

Then I had plenty of time to relax and think about my relationship with Zoo. He was perfect but he had a street attachment that was coming between us. I always knew it would be a problem in the back of my head, but I tried to give him the benefit of the doubt. That shit came back to bite me in the ass like a boomerang. I knew he wasn't hearing me yet about getting out of the streets, but I wasn't gon' give up trying to talk some sense into him.

"You good, bae? I know it's a lot, but please, please, please, just bear with me," Zoo said.

"I promise you, it's good. There's nothing wrong with you taking care of your family, babe."

He licked his lips. "Damn, how did I get this lucky?" I couldn't do anything but giggle and kiss him.

When I got back home from vacation, I was surprised to see Zoo's son and mama here. He told me they had to stay there for a while because a lot was going on. I guess he thought I would be tripping, but it actually warmed my heart. He was becoming the father that his son needed, and his relationship with his mother was rocky but I had a feeling that it would get better with time.

I had to admit, the situations were crazy. I couldn't believe that a seven-year-old was capable of so much. He wanted to be Zoo so badly. Everything that he was trying to prevent was coming to existence. That was another reason for him to get out of the streets. His son wanted to do the exact same thing his daddy was known for. He ain't playing that bullshit with Hendrix though. He had his lil' ass on a short leash. As he should.

Now the whole situation with Sharonda shocked me the most. I didn't even have much to say to Zoo when he told me about her. I told him about our encounter in the grocery store and he just shook his head. But when Zoo formally introduced us when I got back, it was like her mind went blank. She didn't even remember the run-in from the store. She still remembered who I was because of Kareem, but that was it. Zoo said that she didn't remember the situation from stabbing that teenager either.

And even though I had to serve her ass in the grocery store a while back, I told Zoo I would help him with her. He truly needed it. He was pissed, stressed, and exhausted. I told him he needed a "me time" vacation next. He wasn't going for it, just like I knew he wouldn't. Zoo always carried the weight of the world on his shoulders. That's all he ever knew.

Bzzt. Bzzt. Bzzt. That was the third time that Zoo's phone had gone off this morning and he ignored the call. The calls were from somebody named "L." And I could tell when a man was trying to hide something. His whole body language changed. And I had already been noticing shit was off with him anyways. I couldn't help but say something. But first I had to get my ducks in order before a nigga lied.

"Can you wire two hundred thousand dollars into my account?" I asked.

I hardly ever asked Zoo for anything and to be asking for such a large amount of money was bold. I thought he was gon' look at me sideways or ask 'for what,' but he didn't. He called the bank and had them honor his request in five minutes. I checked my account and it was there, every penny. I was impressed.

"You need anything else?" he asked. Straight like that, he didn't flinch or shit.

"No, I'm good. I only asked for that in case I need to leave yo' ass for cheating on me with whoever keeps blowing up yo' fucking phone!"

"How you gon' sit here and trip on me after all that good ass dick I gave you?"

"And how you gon' sit up here and play in my face like I'm stupid? I know when a nigga is creeping on me. Yo' ass been acting funny and I'm just tryna see what's up, 'cause me and my son can bounce."

Oh, he was pissed then. He hopped out of the bed and slid his white tee over his head. "All of a sudden I'm cheating 'cause my phone rang. We were good just five minutes ago and now yo' insecurities showing."

"Insecurities, huh? You can't even deny the shit or tell me who's calling you. But I'd bet two hundred thousand dollars that you're putting on clothes to go and see why that bitch keeps calling you. All I'mma say is, let me find out," I snapped.

He slid his feet into his white Air Forces and pulled his hair back with a scrunchie. "You got it all wrong. But you can think what you want," he said, leaving.

I wasn't a fool, and I damn sure wasn't about to sit still while this nigga did his dirt. I always had the feeling that maybe he was cheating, but I kept thinking, *nah, he's too good to me to do that.* I didn't know for sure, but I was 99.9 percent sure he was.

And he had me all the way fucked up if he didn't think I wouldn't follow him. I told Sharonda I would be back in fifteen minutes and to sit tight with the kids. I almost lost him but he got caught at a red light and I caught up to him. I stayed far back so he wouldn't see me. I wanted to see where his ass was going.

He led me straight to a neighborhood I had never been to. He finally turned into the driveway of the house and got out of the car angry. *Like I said.* He went banging on the door until someone finally answered. I couldn't make out who she was until she turned her head. "Detective Hollis?"

But wait, she looked... different. She was definitely smaller. But that was the least of my worries. I didn't understand why Zoo was meeting up with a cop. The same exact cop that threw me behind bars to be exact. A million thoughts rumbled through my head. *He can't be sleeping with her. I know his ass wouldn't sleep with a cop. So is he snitching? Oh my God, what if he's snitching?*

I quickly sped off with tears in my eyes. I didn't know what to believe. I grabbed my phone from the passenger seat. Then I realized, I had no one to call because my best friend was six feet under.

Sighing, I scrolled to the number that Reem called me from and dialed it. It was good to hear his voice. "Hey, beautiful," he answered.

I rolled my eyes at his compliment. Reem hadn't complimented me in years. It sounded kinda weird hearing him say it. But the only reason why I called him was to get my mind off of what I had recently seen. So I ignored it.

"How's life?" I asked.

"Shit, rough. But I ain't really trying to complain. I brought this shit on myself so I'm surviving."

"I know the feeling," I said.

The line grew quiet. "Everything good? Is Kamara's death on your mind? I know something has to be wrong if you're calling me," he said with a little chuckle.

"To be honest, Reem, I don't even wanna talk about me right now. Make me laugh. I need it," I said.

"Do you wanna hear a funny but not so funny story about Kamara?" he asked.

"Funny story? Y'all barely got along. I need to know what funny story y'all shared," I said with a little chuckle. It was the thought of Kamara that made me laugh already. Her ass was so damn mean.

"Nah, I never really got along with Kamara, but I was glad you had her. She had your back with everything that I put you through. She stood ten toes behind you every time. Even when you went to jail behind my bullshit, she stayed down. Her crazy ass caught me slipping in the parking lot of Family Dollar. She pulled up fast as hell and blocked me in. She hopped out of the car on ten! Oh, she was mad as fuck behind you. She told me off, beat my ass, and then left."

When Kareem said that shit, I was laughing my ass off. 'Cause what, Kamara? My girl did not play about me at all. I was laughing so hard that my stomach started hurting. She never told me that she beat Kareem's ass. God I felt bad for how things ended. *Damn, why the fuck did I have to lose my best friend?*

"You okay, baby?"

"I'm so glad you told me about that, Kareem. That shit was funny. But tell me about you now and...your life in prison," I said.

"You'll probably say I'm stupid for this, but I joined a gang. I only joined for protection though. They were beating my ass before but now I've been making a way. I know you think it's all bad because I said I'm part of a gang but... it's really not. I've learned more here than I learned on the outside. Respect, I never gave you that. Loyalty, I never gave you that. Trust, I never gave you a reason to. It may sound crazy, but sometimes I think it was meant for me to die but I just keep dodging these crazy ass bullets."

I giggled. "That's because you're a lucky ass nigga. But seriously, Reem, if you were meant to be dead, you would be dead, so just stop talking like that," I said.

"I guess, but look, I gotta go. Kiss baby boy for me. I love you."

"Okay."

CHAPTER FIFTEEN
ZACHARY "ZOO" SLAID

"I don't understand why you're tripping about me calling you all of a sudden. We're supposed to be business partners. You didn't give a damn about me calling you at any time when your son was missing," Lenoir cried.

"We were business partners, nothing more, nothing less. But you can cancel that shit. Yo' ass buggin', for real," I shot back.

"Bugging because I called you to discuss business? And you are not leaving me with this. This shit has been tucked in my house for over a month, Zoo. We need to move it," she hollered.

She was right, but that wasn't the reason why her ass was blowing me up. I had too much on my plate. I wasn't about to drown myself deeper in the game. "Nah, you bugging 'cause this shit ain't about making money. You prancing around here with this plastic body, looking like a knock-off version of my girl. Fuck you talm 'bout, Lenoir? I got enough problems. You ain't 'bout to be another one."

She smacked her lips and popped her hip. "So now it's fuck me but when you need me, you can put in favors at any time."

"Look, I'll help you get this shit out ya place but after that, we done, yo. I don't want any dealings," I reasoned.

I tried to walk around her, but she grabbed me. "Why?!" She pushed me and I grabbed her arms.

"Don't put yo' fucking hands on me!"

"You owe me an explanation. I have stuck my neck out for you countless times and I even quit my job for you," she cried.

"Bih, what?! Oh, you tripping for real. I'mma bounce before I say some shit to hurt yo' feelings." I grabbed my keys from the table. "I'mma set some moves up for you and Chip to move that weight. Me and you, we're done." I pointed between the two of us.

I felt bad making shorty cry, but she was fucking up my life more. I had to put a stop to that shit before I got in too deep. I got in my ride and took my ass home. I was relieved to see Ryah's car still home. I was lowkey worried she would leave me. But all I needed for her to do was give me time. I was getting my affairs in order. The process was just moving a lot... slower than what I hoped. I just had to tell her that it was a possibility that Hero was my kid, handle the situation with Sharonda, make sure Ro didn't hit rock bottom, and keep Hendrix in line.

Using my key, I let myself inside. Sharonda was on the couch leaning over a trash can. That detox was eating her ass up. We hardly ever shared any words in passing. I still hadn't gotten used to the idea of seeing her so often yet. My OG would be happy to know that Sharonda had moved in with me, but her memory was worsening as time passed.

I passed her without a word and went up the stairs to look for Ryah. She was sitting in the middle of our bed, folding clothes. The regret hit me as soon as my eyes met hers and I felt her pain. I was wrong for how I came at her earlier but damn, a nigga was stressed.

"I think I owe you an apology," I said, licking my lips.

"No, I think you owe me the truth," she snapped.

Then out of nowhere, Sharonda started screaming my name. Everybody ran to see what was going on with her. She stood with her hands tucked in between her legs. Blood leaked down her legs and she held her stomach in pain.

Jase started crying from all of the commotion. Ryah tried consoling him and Hendrix just stood there. I rushed over to her side to help hold her up. She dug her nails into my shoulder blade every time a wave of pain came over her.

I told Ryah to stay back with the kids while I took her to the hospital, but she wasn't hearing that. She put the kids in a separate car and followed close behind. Sharonda cried like somebody was ripping her apart the entire ride to the hospital.

The more she cried, the more it fucked with me. We didn't have the best relationship, but I couldn't stand to see her in so much pain. Her clothes were drenched in blood and so were my seats. She couldn't walk so I had to carry her inside. She weighed no more than a feather, even while pregnant.

"Help! Help!" I yelled.

A couple of paramedics were leaning against the wall chatting. Once they noticed us, they ran over. I placed her on the gurney and they rolled her to the back. A light tap on the shoulder caused me to turn around, and it was Ryah.

"Should I call the family?" she asked.

Damn. I hadn't even thought about that shit. My mind had been so preoccupied that I hadn't even told my OG or my aunts that Sharonda was expecting twins.

"Yeah, take care of that for me," I said.

While Ryah took care of calling everybody, I got the boys settled in the waiting room. I sat next to Ryah and laid my head back against the wall with my eyes closed. Thoughts of Hero crossed my mind. I wondered what he was like. Of course, we met and spent a day together at the carnival, but I hadn't been able to get to know him yet. I was already learning about his bad ass brother.

Hendrix was coming along though. After Chip showed him what the streets were like, he straightened his act up real quick. He'd been asking to go back with his mama but I wouldn't let him. He only wanted to go with her because I wouldn't let his lil' ass have no phone or any other electronics. The only thing his lil' ass had been able to do was read books, color, and run around outside a little.

"Family of Slaid," a doctor called out.

This shit felt all too familiar. Me and Ryah walked over to meet the doctor while the boys sat in their seats.

"Ms. Slaid is doing well." Relief came over me. "But she did deliver the babies and I'm sorry to say, but they were stillborn."

Was it bad that I felt no type of way when he said that? Sharonda wasn't equipped for more children. She could barely take care of herself let alone two babies.

"Can we see her?" I asked.

"Of course. But if you don't mind, I would like to suggest rehab. She needs professional help and from what I've learned, you're her son," he said.

"Rehab? She ain't gon' do that shit. She gon' drop out and get back on the streets again. It's a waste of fucking money," I snapped.

"Well, has she ever been in rehab before?"

"Nah, but all she knows is the streets," I said.

"You've never given her the opportunity, so you wouldn't

know. But I can only make a suggestion. You can follow me and I'll take you to her room," he said.

We followed him back to Sharonda's room. She was laid in the bed looking like straight hell. She was sad. I could see it from her worn eyes. The longer I sat there and stared, I felt bad. It was time for me to man up and stop holding onto pain, anger, and resentment.

"What was that you were saying about rehab, Doc?" I turned and asked.

He smiled and welcomed me to his office while Ryah and the kids sat with Sharonda. As I followed behind him, a sense of peace came over me. I couldn't help but smile. I was proud of myself. I never pictured the day that I would put my hatred for her behind me and move forward. I could feel myself becoming a better man.

"You can have a seat there and I'll grab some forms so we can look them over, and if you decide to commit then we can make something happen," he said.

"Fasho. Fasho."

"Do you have any questions for me?" he asked as he rambled through his file cabinet.

"I mean, I thought you were gon' explain the process to me," I said.

He chuckled. "Of course. So, first thing is first, your mother—"

"Just Sharonda for now, please," I said, cutting him off.

"Okay, well Sharonda needs to detox. She'll be assigned a therapist, an assessment and checkup are completed, and she'll be admitted into our program. Medical detox will begin if necessary at this point. Once detox is complete, we can move her to residential care where she will continue to have the support of our 24-hour medical supervision while receiving intense therapy and additional services offered. She will go through steps through this process and they are all listed in this brochure," he said. He handed me a brochure.

I opened it up and skimmed through it. "And how long is rehab?"

"There is no set period. We assess every patient individually and throughout their plan of care we determine their progress," he shared.

"Aite, fasho. How do I sign her up?"

"We can start on that right now, but first we need to speak about the form of payment. I saw in Ms. Slaid's chart that she doesn't have any medical insurance, which is okay. We have financing programs to help out with costs."

"No need for that, Doc. I can pay for it all right now." I reached into my pocket and pulled out my wallet. "We can set up everything. Charge the full amount, I'm good for it," I said.

"Don't you want to know the total, Mr. Slaid?" he asked.

"Heh, nah, I'm good man. Just tell me where I can sign so I can get her the proper help she needs."

He had a Kool-Aid smile on his face. "Let's get started then."

* * *

"Look, Sharonda, I can't keep letting this shit go on. You need help. More help than what I can provide at my home. I signed you up for rehab... Just please, do this one thing for me. One thing, that's all I ask," I said to Sharonda.

She looked like she was on her deathbed. I guess her giving birth caused a toll on her body, because she looked even worse than before.

"I'm sorry, Zoo. I failed you and here you are helping me. I wish I would've been the mother you deserved. I'm glad Mama was there to right my wrongs... I have never been to rehab before, but I promise to try my best. I love you." She closed her eyes, and I didn't know if she fell asleep or if she was just resting her eyes.

I didn't even know what to say anyways. She threw me all the way off with that one.

CHAPTER SIXTEEN

SAVANNAH GOOD

COURT DAY

Ever since I told my therapist what actually happened, my life changed drastically. I was immediately moved to a holding room where I was questioned for hours. I hated it. They judged me, all of them. I could feel it, but they didn't know my pain. They didn't even try to understand what I was going through. Once they got what they needed, they hung my ass out to dry.

I'm talking about, they absolutely hated me and gave me no sympathy for abandoning my daughter. I didn't expect them to, but I didn't expect them to drill me either.

Then there were my parents who were breathing down my neck. They wanted me to care so badly, but I didn't. Yeah, I felt better after telling them what happened, but nothing would bring Maya back.

My parents went all out and got me the best lawyer money could pay for. And my people were pretty wealthy. They weren't rich but they both had money. My mother was a urologist and my father owned a welding company. And I could tell they paid top dollar for my attorney.

He sported a black, tailored Giorgio Armani suit and red-bottom shoes that cost more than triple my old rent. He was groomed well, no facial hair and a cute left dimple. He looked to be in his mid-thirties. Hmm, a cute white boy.

But I hoped he was as smart as he was cute. He managed to have my court date moved from two years out to now. He said the prosecutor was anxious to put me behind bars for my actions and so was the DA. He signed off on a waiver to have my court date moved up.

It was a good and a bad thing. Good for my parents because they didn't want me sitting in a psych ward for two years, waiting for my court date. It was bad because everybody was against me and they were coming hard. The likelihood of me being convicted was high. That's why my lawyer had been practicing mock trials in the courthouse with me all morning. Court was scheduled for 2 p.m. and we had been prepping for hours, and it was now time.

He was confident, whereas I really didn't know what to do with my emotions. I was wrong for what I did to my daughter. I shouldn't have abandoned her. I blamed myself for sticking around with Reem's no-good ass when the signs were there. And because I ignored my instincts, our daughter was killed. I deserved punishment for all of it. I wouldn't feel right just walking away freely. I don't know what my fate should be. Everybody had a different opinion of me.

"Are you okay, baby?" my mother questioned.

She used the back of her hand to stroke the side of my face. I shrugged because I wasn't in much of a mood to talk. My mind was all over the place. One minute I was thinking about my daughters, then the next I was thinking about my life, and eventually I would snap back into reality and focus on the trial my lawyer was preparing me for.

I had no faith in him at all. He had me dolled up in a yellow floral dress and my hair in spunky curls. He said that it would warm the jury and have them look at me in the eye of a mother. It was all bullcrap to me. Those people were only gonna care about one thing, if he could make it seem like I was a good person.

"I know it's tough, Vannah, but we need you to be strong here," my father said. "We are right along with you. We don't blame you, sweetheart. We are trying to help you, but you have to wanna help yourself first. Help us help you," he continued.

I took a breath and shook my head. "Okay, Daddy."

We went over our strategy a few more times, then it was time for the rest of my future to be determined.

2 p.m. - Court

There were a plethora of things running through my head as I followed behind my attorney, Mr. Bowman, into the courtroom. *What does everyone think of me? Do they think I'm a bad mother? I wish I could just hide under a rock.* All of those thoughts ran through my head, making me uneasy. It wasn't until I got a glance at the prosecutor that I became completely intimidated. He was frightening and looked to be about his business. I was too afraid to even look at the jury. I kept my head low and followed the instructions Mr. Bowman had given me.

"All rise! Department One of the Superior Court is now in session. Judge Miranda presiding. Please be seated," the bailiff said.

Everyone in the courtroom stood to their feet in respect of the judge. The courtroom was cold, quiet, and full of people.

"Good morning, ladies and gentlemen. Calling the case of the People of the State of Georgia versus Savannah Good. Are both sides ready?" the judge asked.

"Ready for the people, Your Honor," the district attorney replied.

"Ready for the defense, Your Honor," Mr. Bowman said.

The judge nodded and the clerk swore in the jury. The deputy district attorney stood up first for the opening statement.

"Your Honor, and ladies and gentlemen of the jury, the defendant has been charged with abandonment of a minor and child abuse in the form of neglect." He grabbed the remote and pointed it toward a projector screen. There were pictures of Blessing, dirty from poop and vomit. And her eyes were puffy from continuously crying. I turned my head in shame. "When employers found the child, she was soiled and starving. The evidence will show that Ms. Good is unfit and is a danger to herself, her child, and society," he continued.

"Objection, Your Honor, that's speculation. My client poses no threat to anyone," Mr. Bowman interrupted.

"Sustained," said the judge.

The prosecutor continued on to the jury. "The evidence I present will prove to you that the defendant is guilty as charged."

Mr. Bowman looked over at me, insinuating that it was time. I sat up and moved my curls behind my ear. "Your Honor, and ladies and gentlemen of the jury, under the law, my client is presumed innocent until proven guilty. During this trial, you will hear no real evidence against her. You will come to know the truth that Savannah here had a moment of vulnerability and her mental health got the best of her. Therefore, my client is not guilty."

"The prosecution may call its first character witness," Judge Miranda said.

The prosecutor smiled arrogantly and glanced over at us. I

dropped my head and fiddled with the rim of my dress. "The People call Carla Banks to the stand," he said.

That caught my attention. *Kareem's mom? She's testifying against me?* I looked over at my lawyer to see his reaction. He didn't flinch. I thought he would be moved since we didn't discuss Kareem's mother testifying during mock trials. I guess it was all part of his 'plan.'

Mrs. Banks made her way to the stand. She looked like a species of apes from *Animal Planet*. I never knew her like that. We had dealings with each other a few times, but that was because it was something involving Maya. And Reem was always there. She knew absolutely nothing about me, so I didn't understand why they were calling her to the stand.

"Mrs. Banks, how do you know the defendant?" the prosecutor asked.

She looked over at me with the stank face. "She was my son's side piece before he left her when she went crazy," she said. The jury gasped.

"Objection, Your Honor, can we refrain from the use of derogatory names about my client? That's defamation," Mr. Bowman spoke up.

"Sustained, the witness will refer to the defendant by her name," he said.

The prosecutor continued. "And what do you know about Savannah, Ms. Banks?"

"She is the mother of two of my grandkids. My poor grandbaby died in a fire in her care. Then this crazy chick abandoned my grandbaby when my son was trying to take care of her. I forgot to mention that she also abandoned Blessing at the hospital too. She didn't even give her a name. My son had been taking care of Blessing. She ended up in her care when she had him arrested on false charges. This sick girl left my newborn granddaughter in a filthy bathroom on a fast food restaurant floor. She is no type of a mother," she said.

My attorney didn't lie when he said they would try to destroy my character first. He said they would do that so the jury would depict an image of me in their heads. I knew it worked because I felt ashamed. Almost everything she said was right about me. And I say almost because I was never a nigga's side bitch. That nigga lied to me like I was his only girl, and his bitch ass was cheating. Whew, that struck a nerve in me. I wanted to slap that nappy ass wig off of her head for coming for me.

"No further questions, Your Honor."

"Would the defense like to cross examine?" the judge asked.

"We would, Your Honor," Mr. Bowman responded. "Mrs. Banks, you referred to my client as a 'side piece' when in fact, your son, Kareem Banks, had a relationship with Savannah and another young woman at the same time. These women supported and took care of your fully grown son, but he was the downfall to both of these young women's lives. And if you don't remember, I'll jog your memory," he said with a wink.

He grabbed documents from our table and handed them to the judge as he spoke. "Kareem Banks is currently serving a forty-one-year sentence for murder, armed robbery of a bank, and kidnapping of a minor. He murdered the sister of my client, Quesha Good, and kidnapped—"

"Your Honor, objection. Kareem Banks isn't on trial here. The defense is getting off topic," the prosecutor interjected.

"Sustained. Stay on topic, counselor," she warned.

"The defense rests," Mr. Bowman said.

"The witness is excused," said Judge Miranda. "Does the defense wish to ask any questions?" she continued.

"Yes, Your Honor."

"The defense calls Tanya Reyes to the stand," he said.

My stomach turned when he called her name. I didn't care for her anymore after she gave me up. Of course, I knew she couldn't keep my secrets, but because of her—who was I kidding? I was sitting in my predicament because of me, nobody else.

"Mrs. Reyes, could you please state your relation to the court?"

"Of course, I was the defendant's therapist while she was in holding. I worked alongside a psychiatrist and psychologist in her treatment," she said.

Mr. Bowman took more documents from his briefcase and handed them to Judge Miranda. "And from your team's expert opinion, what was the conclusion after carefully evaluating my client?" he asked.

She looked over at me with a warm smile. "Savannah Good is one of the most pleasant patients I have ever worked with. You see, what happened to Savannah was a domino effect that led to her actions with her daughter, Blessing. The day that Blessing was born was the same day that Savannah lost her daughter in a tragic fire. Her then boyfriend was also trapped inside the house with her daughter, but he was enjoying sexual encounters with her sister and wasn't able to save their daughter." My parents dropped their heads and wiped tears from their eyes. "Savannah never had time to grieve the death of her daughter before being given the role of motherhood again. Savannah never caused any physical harm to Blessing. She left her in a bathroom in a restaurant after realizing that she couldn't care for Blessing. Not in a sense of abandonment but in a sense of a psychotic break. After careful evaluation, my team and I ruled that Savannah Good was under a state of temporary insanity in the act of the crime," she said.

"And can you explain to the court what temporary insanity is?" Mr. Bowman asked.

"Yes, temporary insanity is when the patient is not capable of distinguishing right and wrong during the crime."

"No further questions," he said.

The prosecutor stood to his feet. "Your Honor, the People rest their case."

"Does the defense rest?" questioned Judge Miranda.

"Yes, Your Honor," Mr. Bowman answered.

Judge Miranda spoke to the jury regarding the jury instructions and prompted the prosecutor and Mr. Bowman for the final arguments. The prosecutor was first to address the jury.

"Your Honor, and ladies and gentlemen of the jury, there is no excuse for the defendant's actions. At any time she could have utilized the state's Safe Haven Laws and left the infant at a church, hospital, or fire station. Leaving a child on the floor in a bathroom isn't insanity, it's unfit and neglect. She does not deserve to walk the streets of Atlanta after her actions. Based on the evidence, you must find the defendant guilty," he said.

My attorney chuckled under his breath after the prosecutor finished. Then he took the floor.

"Your Honor, ladies and gentlemen of the jury, the pain of losing a child is something that no one should have to experience. Most of us are familiar with postpartum depression. She was robbed of all happiness and couldn't cope with all of the mixed emotions. The DA is trying to make my client look like a monster when she's a model citizen. Before this incident, my client has never been in any kind of trouble. This was unfortunate, and my client ended up with the short end of the stick. She would never purposely harm her children. That means that there is reasonable doubt; therefore, you must find her not guilty," he said.

After the last statements were given, the jury was escorted

to the back and I grew nervous. I tapped my foot impatiently against the floor as I waited. I know I said I didn't care before, but as I sat through trial, I realized I wasn't the person they were trying to make me out to be. I needed help, better help than what a jailed facility could provide.

After what felt like hours, the jury made their way back to the stand. I actually couldn't believe a bunch of strangers who didn't know me would be determining my future.

"Will the foreperson of the jury please stand? Have you reached a verdict?" the judge asked.

An older Hispanic guy stood to his feet. "Yes, Your Honor."

"Will the defendant please stand? You may read the verdict," she directed.

"The jury finds the defendant not guilty by reason of temporary insanity."

I could hear my mother shout out from behind me, and I turned to look at my family. My mama had her hands over her chest. My daddy's face was glistening with tears. They were so happy and I was too. Finally, court was adjourned and they allowed us to rejoice together.

* * *

"I can't believe you moved back to Georgia, Daddy. Where have you been staying?" I asked my father.

"After everything that was going on with you and your sister, how could I not move back for my children, Vannah?" He turned and sat his mug of coffee on the counter. "Sweetheart, your mother and I are still processing everything. We lost a daughter, a granddaughter, and almost you. I've been staying in a hotel, but I think I'm going to stay with you until everything gets a little better around here," he continued.

We were standing in the middle of my kitchen and it felt

like a dream. I had prepared myself to stay locked away, and I blocked out all thoughts of my home. My daddy told me he had been paying the lights and the bills because he had faith that I would be home soon.

"So you're not mad about the...Quesha situation?" I asked.

I was nervous about bringing up my sister's name. My feelings about her death were indifferent, but I knew my parents felt differently. As they should. They lost a child and I, for one, can vouch for the amount of pain that entails.

And I didn't make it better with all of the mental shit I had going on. I was ashamed for even allowing myself to get to that point. I was never that person, allowing myself to get caught slipping. And growing up, I was a happy child. Both me and my sister. We were spoiled. I never had any mental issues. Something inside of me just broke that day and I snapped.

"None of that was your fault, sweetheart. We knew all along that you didn't hurt Quesha. We don't blame you for anything. The only important thing right now is getting you help," he said.

"Help? When you say help, what do you mean? I don't want to be locked in a facility anymore," I said.

"Not a facility but you will receive outpatient care. Your mother has already set you up to see a psychiatrist at the hospital she works at. You're gonna see her once a week and I'm going to be here for you as well," he said. I sighed and took a seat on the bar stool. "It's gonna get better, baby girl. Think about Blessing," he continued.

"Sorry, Daddy, I just can't think about the child that I abandoned and lost custody of."

"Savannah, your mother was awarded custody from the state when they found Blessing." I snapped my neck to him. "The social workers asked us not to inform you until after the case. And right now, they have it restricted so you can't see her.

But that's just the beginning, Vannah. We're gonna work through this together and eventually, you will gain rights back to her... But only when you're ready," he said.

I started to pitch a fit, but I didn't even have the energy. I gave up. I let go of all the negative energy trapped inside of my body. I released all of the hate flowing through me. I gave my daddy a chance. "Okay, Daddy."

CHAPTER SEVENTEEN
KAREEM "REEM" BANKS

J ust when a nigga finally started to get in good with my blood brothers, the warden came with his bullshit. Nigga woke me up early this morning so I could see him in his office. And it's rare to see Top walk the halls, so when I saw the nigga staring over my bed, I knew I was still in hot water.

I thought for sure I had gotten off easy with the guard situation when Top let me go back to my cell and I didn't hear anything else about it. Of course, I heard the rumors and whispers around the prison but nothing that had me shook.

Last I heard, they were still investigating. And Slug told me not to worry because they didn't have any hard evidence. That's why no one had gon' down for it yet. Honestly, I didn't give a fuck if I went down for it or not since a nigga was gon' be sitting in prison for life. I just didn't wanna spend the rest of my time locked up in solitary. But overall, I had no more fucks to give.

"Get up! I want you in my office now," he demanded.

Shaking my head, I couldn't believe he was waking me up out of my sleep with the shits. I rubbed my hand down my face then flipped the covers back. I stared at my hard dick momentarily. He needed some attention. I hadn't felt pussy in two fucking months. Shit was miserable. I was horny as fuck and I didn't even have money on my books to buy some lotion. And I couldn't bother Slug with my problems. He had done enough. Plus, no money meant personal problems, and I didn't want Slug looking into my personal life.

After sliding my white tee over my head, I slid my feet into my rubber slides. I didn't have the choice of brushing my teeth and washing my face. The guard shoved me out of my cell and slammed the door behind us.

I stayed quiet, though, I didn't make a fuss. I learned to keep my head down and observe niggas. And I didn't want any enemies, especially a guard. Before, running my mouth only got me in situations I couldn't get out of. The importance of silence was underrated. I was learning quickly though.

We made it to the warden's office and he had the guard leave us be. I mentally prepared myself for this nigga because I knew he was coming with some bullshit. I took a seat across from him and he stood behind his desk.

"I know you killed one of my men, Banks. And I know why. But I'm offering you a way out here," he said.

I chuckled. I ran my hand over my hair and down my face. I didn't have waves anymore. My hair had grown a few inches. My shit was curling up.

"I see you laughing, but you haven't heard my offer yet. And you might wanna listen," he threatened.

I leaned back and gestured my hand for him to continue. "We can look past this whole ordeal if you consider being an inside man for me. You know, something like an informant on the guys around here. And I'll look out for you and make sure you don't go down for the guard incident. And I'll make sure you're protected. You already know what will happen if the other guards find out who really did it. I'm looking out for you, son. Oh, and, you won't have to worry about money being on your books because you'd have full access to the commissary. No charge. Think about it."

"I thought about it. I'm good."

"Just like that? No hesitation?" he questioned.

"And it's gon' stay like that. Do what you gotta do, Top." I shrugged my shoulders.

He crossed his arms over his chest and smiled. "Slug was right about you. You might just be the man we need for the job," he said.

Scrunching up my face, I was confused. "Job?"

Then, in walked Slug, no guard escort or nun. He slapped hands with Top and it was the official Blood handshake. My eyes widened at what I was witnessing.

"Yo, what the fuck is going on?" I asked.

Slug smiled. "Calm down, pretty boy. It's all good. You just earned my respect for life. We had to test yo' ass to see if you were down with us for real or if you were just using us. But you stood solid and now we can let you in on our operation around here," Slug said with mischievous eyes.

"Operation?"

"Yeh. You see, me and Top are Blood brothers and we run drugs through the Georgia Prison Systems." I sat up in my seat. "And you just earned your keep," he said.

Internally, I smiled and felt like a lil' ass kid graduating from preschool. But externally, I kept a straight face and nodded. I was thrown by everything when he hit me with that curve ball. I thought for sure I was going down for a guard's murder, but these niggas set all of this shit up to see if I was pussy or not. And if I would've snitched, they would've killed me dead.

"So what now?" I asked.

I thought bro was gon' tell me what the operation entailed, but it was more to it. I was a part of the fucking operation. These niggas had a whole plan.

"Top's gon' set up a temporary transfer for you to another prison in Georgia. On transport day, you'll swallow balloons of drugs before they load you up. When you get to the prison and process in, that's when you'll vomit the balloons back up. They will pat you down to make sure you don't have any weapons, and that's when you'll ask to go to the bathroom. One of the guards will escort you but they don't go inside. Once you get inside, the second stall on the left has a vent above the toilet. Get 'em out and put them inside. After a few days of being there, Top will tell them that there was an issue with paperwork and you will be transferred back," Slug said.

"Nigga, what? Did you forget that I still have to go to the infirmary every couple of days to get my bandages changed from previous injuries? My body will never be able to handle holding drugs," I said.

"Too bad I wasn't asking. I tried to make it easier on—"

"Aite, I'm in," I said, cutting him off.

Another smile crept over his face. "Aite then. That's a bet." He grabbed me by the shoulders with his heavy hands. "And you know I always look out, my boy. After you serve at least a few years in this dump, Top is gon' recommend good shit to the parole board. We gon' deposit money into an account for you every month. You can use that shit for your family back home or whatever. And not only that, you're gon' get your own individual cell on B-block. Oh, and we got pussy for days if you don't have a special lady back home. Top can set that up for you too. We got bitches that we slide a few bills their way and then we pound their ass any way we like on conjugal visit days."

"W-w-wait. Pussy and money?"

"Nah, pussy, money, and power. You gotta look at the bigger picture, my boy."

"Let's do it."

CHAPTER EIGHTEEN
SKYLER SINCLAIR

After spending five hours setting up for a birthday party alone, I was tired. I should've listened to my mama when she told me to hire someone. I wanted to do something different for my boys, so I tried decorating for Hero's fifth birthday party myself. Everything came out a success, but I was tired as fuck from carrying a hundred items from the car and up the elevator. I must've taken at least fifteen trips.

And my baby was so grateful. When he saw the ninja turtle decor hanging everywhere, he melted. That made all of my hard work worthwhile. He and his little friends were having a blast. Lord knows I gave the entire kindergarten an invitation. It didn't matter if I decorated or hired a planner, all they cared about was having fun. They enjoyed the ninja turtle playdough the most. Anything that had a ninja turtle logo or picture, I grabbed it. I fucked up a bag in Party City. I had to go all out for my boy.

And, of course, my overgrown seven-year-old thought the party was too childish for him. He stood around like a chaperone for the kids. Since staying with Zoo, his behavior had changed drastically. He was more respectful and his teachers said he was doing much better in school. Since he was doing so well, I decided to let him continue to stay with Zoo.

I picked up Hendrix for the party after I was done with everything. I didn't tell Zoo about the party though. That was a battle I didn't feel like dealing with.

"Hey Skyler, where can I put Hero's gift?" one of the parents asked.

"You can put it on the table next to the treat table," I said, pointing.

He had hella presents too. I didn't expect him to get so much stuff. The love surrounding my son was enormous. He had friends and family that loved him to death, he wasn't missing out on anything with Zoo not being around. He had his village.

"I feel for you when you have to clean all of this stuff up," my mama said from behind.

I turned around to face her. "I know right. It'll probably take me about three days," I said.

I tried to walk away, but my mama grabbed my hand. "Not today, Mama. I don't wanna hear about Zoo and Hero. I'm grown and I can handle my own life. Leave it alone," I said in aggravation.

Today was not the day for one of her motherly speeches. I turned on my heels and went off to check on Hendrix. I hadn't seen him in a while and I needed to make sure he wasn't getting into any trouble. And my mind started to wander when I couldn't find him anywhere. I checked all of the rooms in the house and pool area and there was no sign of him.

Hero ran past me and I grabbed him by his arm. "Have you seen your brother?" I asked.

"Yes, Mommy, he's in the closet calling Daddy to tell him about the party," he said.

"Ughhhhh!"

I stormed off in the direction of Hendrix's room. His ass was hard headed because I told him not to tell his daddy anything about this party. I burst into his closet and snatched the phone from his hand. He was using Hero's phone. And I got there right on time because he was in the middle of the call with his daddy. I clicked the end button and went in on his lil' ass.

"What did I tell you? Why would you call your daddy when I told you not to?" I chastised him.

"I know, Mama, but Hero wanted Daddy to be here. I knew you wouldn't call him."

I pinched the bridge of my nose and closed my eyes momentarily. I had to find some peace before I ended up jacking that lil' boy up.

I grabbed him by his face. "When I tell you not to do something, I mean it," I scolded.

I wanted to go in more, but I couldn't beat my other child down the hallway from my guests. He got the message though. I was tired of his lil' ass. I interlocked my hand with his and we went back to the party to sing happy birthday.

But to my surprise, they were already singing it and Zoo was there leading everything along. Stopping in my tracks, my body fumed with anger. I must've grown the devil horns because when we made eye contact, he already knew what it was. He sat Hero down in the chair and came over to where I was.

Because I didn't wanna cause a scene in front of everyone, we took the conversation to my bedroom.

"What the fuck do you think you're doing?!"

"Bruh, you dumb as fuck! How—"

Pushing him in his chest, I screamed, "No, I'm hurt! For years, all I wanted you to do is get out of the streets and become a father to our son, but you just couldn't do it. You thought your money would be good enough for your absence. And he still turned out to be the spawn of Chucky. But that's not even the point. It's the fact that the second you meet somebody 'special' you decide to turn your whole life around like my son hasn't needed you for seven years. That shit hurts, Zoo! My son deserved his daddy."

He grabbed my hands and looked into my eyes. Ugh, I hated him. "Sky... you right. I should've manned up and got out of the streets for my son. When Zaryah came along, she gave me more of a push to do that. I ain't making excuses, because you're right. But it ain't shit that I can do to change that. I'm just trying to be a better father to my son or sons. We need to move past this shit. Why you punishing Hero because of some shit that you're holding onto? Pull yo' fucking panties up and put your hate to the side. If he's mine, I'm gon' be in his life. This shit ends today," he spat.

Slap! Zoo grabbed my hands and I saw fire in his eyes. I didn't back down though. "Don't ever put yo' fucking hands on me, Sky!" he growled.

I had no more fucks to give. I wasn't a fighter, but he had crossed the line. I drew my fist back, swung, and he ducked. He scooped me up and slammed me on the bed. He grabbed me by the throat and squeezed until I couldn't breathe. I kicked and punched his ass, but he was stronger than me. He let go of my neck and pinned my arms down and locked his legs with my legs with mine. "Sky, chill out before I fuck you up! I'm giving yo' ass chances," he spat.

Finally freeing one of my legs, I kneed him in the balls, causing him to free me. "Ahhh! Fuck!" he groaned.

I hopped up quickly and started swinging my arms wildly. I

was hitting him all over and ripping his shirt to pieces. My long acrylic nails scratched up his body. He placed both of his arms around me and held me in a bear hug. I used my head to hit his lip, and he dropped me. He was trying his hardest not to hit me, and he got angrier the more physical I got.

I knew I had hit the last straw though. He locked his eyes on me and dropped his head to check his lip for blood. My adrenaline was pumping and I was ready for whatever. I was pissed and didn't give a fuck about anything else in that moment. I even grabbed the glass lamp on the end table and busted it on his head.

The impact from the lamp didn't stop him, but it did daze him a little. He stumbled backward, knocking the TV off the stand. He blinked repeatedly, trying to get himself together. He grabbed the back of his head, and he was leaking blood. Reaching behind his back, he grabbed his gun and pointed it at me. By that time, my mother walked in and jumped in front of him.

"What the hell is going on here? Y'all in here fighting like cats and dogs. And boy, if you don't get that gun out of my daughter's face," my mother demanded.

Zoo lowered his gun. "Nah, ya daughter in here going fucking crazy. She better be glad my OG taught me better than hitting a woman or I would've put her ass through this wall," Zoo fussed!

"Really, Zachary? Really, Skyler? Y'all are too grown to be carrying on like this. Skyler, baby, I have told you time after time, let it go. Hendrix and Hero will always be loved whether or not they have a daddy. If he loves some broad more than he loves your sons, then so be it. There is nothing you can do to change that! Fighting him will not change that. You continue to love them indefinitely and move on, baby. It's not worth it," my mama said.

I was still pissed, but my mama was right. Fighting at my five-year-old's birthday party wasn't helping anything. It was making my hate for Zoo grow even more. Zoo tucked his gun back in his pants, and I went to my panty drawer and grabbed the manila folder on top.

Without a word, I walked over and slapped it on Zoo's chest. I gave him the DNA test that he wanted so badly. I got both of my boys tested and they were full Blood brothers, same mother and father. And if that wasn't enough, the lab said he could always come back and give his blood as well.

I stood and watched him open up the folder and read over the documents. "This is all I wanted, Sky." Then he looked at my mother. "And I don't love anybody more than my sons. Don't speak on what you don't know," he said.

"Zoo, really?!" I interjected.

"Fuck this shit, man. I'm out," he said.

I followed him back to the party, and he grabbed Hendrix and left. The parents were side eyeing us because I'm sure we looked crazy. Zoo had scratches all over his face, his shirt was ripped, and I had sweat dripping from my forehead.

I didn't care. My whole mood was fucked up. My mother continued to host the party, and I went back to my room to get myself together.

CHAPTER NINETEEN
LENOIR HOLLIS

"Ninety-seven, ninety-eight, ninety-nine, one hundred. Whew!" I yelled out.

Squats were kicking my ass. I never knew so much came with a BBL. I thought I was good after I had the surgery, but my nurse told me that I had to work out to keep up with the maintenance on my new body.

The waist trainer was what hurt the most. I felt like my insides were being squeezed through the orifices of my body. And honestly, I was only working out to keep my mind off of Zachary Slaid.

I couldn't believe his ass actually had Chip hit me up about our inventory. He's supposed to be in the process of getting a storage unit and moving it next week, but that's beside the point. I hit Zoo's line two times and he never hit me back. I tried to call too, but it went straight to voicemail. I think he had me blocked.

I didn't wanna be the crazy chick that he fucked one time, but he was really making me that way. I felt like he used me until he was done, then he dropped my ass like a bad habit. But

I didn't wanna be done. Zoo never really got to know me for real. All he ever knew was what I could do for him and what my pussy felt like. I knew if he got to know the real me, he would reconsider cutting me off so easily. I had more to offer than just pussy and criminal assistance.

That's why I wasn't giving up on him yet. Until he saw the real Lenoir, I couldn't let him go that easily. And he wasn't making it easy for me. More than likely I was blocked and the likelihood of me seeing him was rare.

I never liked to be a messy bitch, but that time had come. Like I said before, I had come too far to let up now. I had to insert myself into Zoo's personal life to become relevant again. And since me and Zaryah had already crossed paths, I had to take another route. Skyler Sinclair.

I still had all of her information saved into my laptop when I was helping Zoo find his son. I wiped the sweat from my forehead with my towel then grabbed my laptop to do some digging. I took down her address in the notes in my phone and headed in her direction.

I didn't care that I was all sweaty from my mini home workout. I was an angry black woman, ready to raise hell.

"Siri, play 'For Everybody' by Kash Doll," I called out.

"Playing 'For Everybody' by Kash Doll," Siri repeated.

Listen, don't hit my line
Asking why my number in yo' nigga shit
You wasting ya time
Probably shoulda asked that nigga bitch
Probably wouldn't fuck with that
Probably want a bad bitch in his life
I mean, how the fuck am I supposed to know?
I mean, you said that he was yo' nigga right?
Cuffing is dead

You heard what I said, bitch cuffing is dead
These new niggas don't know how to act
They in and out of everybody
Never trust no nigga bitch
All these niggas counterfeit
Baby girl when you gon' learn?
That is not yo' nigga, shit

Finally, coming up to a tall building, I turned my music down to focus better. I couldn't park in the parking garage because it was for owners only. I found a nearby parking lot and I had to pay twenty dollars to park too. Beyond me.

I walked over to the building and I could already tell it was fancy as shit. Any place named Astoria had to be expensive. It had to have at least twenty floors. *Damn, Zoo has them living in a penthouse.* His money was even longer than I thought.

I stepped inside and the lobby area had me in awe. It was black and gold just like my living room decor. The chandelier was the first to draw my attention. God, I could just imagine myself living that lifestyle.

"May I help you, ma'am?" the lobbyman asked.

"Uhm, yes, I was looking for Skyler Sinclair," I said.

"Ms. Sinclair?" He looked over his log. "I don't think she was expecting any visitors. I'll buzz her to let her know she has a visitor though. What's your name?" he asked.

Damn, I thought it would be easier than this. This bitch had to live in a penthouse with top flight security.

"It's Lenoir. Tell her I'm a friend of Zoo's."

"Okay." He smiled.

He buzzed her over the phone and it took him about two minutes to get back with me. He led me to her personal elevator that led to her floor. Baby mama was living lavishly.

What I thought would be a welcoming greeting turned out

to be the total opposite. Homegirl had a gun pointing at me as soon as the elevator opened.

"Who are you and what the fuck do you want with me, 'Zoo's friend'?"

I threw my hands up. "Wait! I just came to chat, that's all. My name is Lenoir Hollis," I said.

"Lenoir?" She lowered her gun. "I heard your name being thrown around when my son was missing," she continued.

Relief came over me. And I had nothing to hide, so I decided to tell her the full truth about everything.

"Can we sit?" I asked.

She waved me over to the couch and I was able to tell her why I came by.

"I'mma just keep it real with you because I'm really at a point now where I'm pissed. So I'll start from the beginning... I used to be a detective and I was investigating Zoo. We couldn't ever pin him on drugs, but then we finally had something when his wife's—"

"Wife?"

"Yeah, he had a wife who stole from him and she ended up dead and we had evidence against one of his homeboys."

She laughed out loud and folded her arms across her chest. "I'm sorry, girl, but this shit is funny as fuck 'cause this nigga is hell. I didn't even know he had a fucking wife. I waited seven whole years for this nigga to grow up and be a part of his son's life. But this nigga didn't even put any thought into my son. He was out getting married and shit and starting a life with bitches, like his son didn't need him here physically," she vented.

Oh, she was hot. I thought she and Zoo had a good relationship, but I was wrong. I was gon' use that to my full advantage. Sis was hurt and I could use her on my team.

"Oh, that's not the end, honey. I had evidence on his friend, but he offered me some dick to keep my mouth closed. I—"

"Baby girl, he finessed the fuck out of you. That dick has powers. That nigga will fuck you so good that you'll wanna marry him the next morning. He played you." She shook her head.

"Girl, that nigga had me quit my job, change up the way I dress, and get my body done. All for him to turn me down for Zaryah Cox." I rolled my eyes.

"Bitch, what? You did all of that for my baby daddy? Yeah, see, you don' bumped yo' damn head. I was just exaggerating when I said you'd wanna marry him. That man used you to the best of his ability and you went out sad over him. But to each his own. If you want a tired ass nigga then girl, more power to you. What made you come here though? I don't get it."

"I really didn't have an agenda when I came over here. He pissed me off and I wanted to make his life hell," I explained.

"Well, you came to the right place 'cause I'm all for it. I got some real tea for you... He just found out my youngest son is his as well, and I doubt he told his lil' girlfriend yet."

Jackpot. I didn't care about anything else she had to say at that point. She had given me the ammo for my gun. I knew this shit here was gon' stir some shit up. Zoo might as well say bye-bye to the old Lenoir because he released a whole new me. They always say, 'a nigga love a toxic bitch.'

But before I left, I had another question for her mad ass. "What's the animosity really about? You wanna get back with him?"

"Not you checking me in my home behind my baby daddy," she laughed. "But honey, I was never with Zoo. We were just fucking around and I got pregnant. It was never that. So to answer your question, I don't want my baby daddy."

"Would you get back with him if he wanted to take it there?" I asked.

"You really want Zoo, huh?" She thought this shit was hilarious. "Listen, baby, Zoo ain't checking for me and I don't want him. And if he did want me, I would never give that man the time of day. I can't forget about seven years of pain. Then I had to learn that he was out here making life changes for bitches over my son. That's unforgivable. My oldest son lives with him now and I just decided to let him start seeing my youngest. Me and Zoo have nothing to discuss but our children," she said.

"I guess." I shrugged. I didn't have any more to talk about with her. She had a smart mouth and I already had gotten what I came for.

"Well, go and fuck it up then, my girl. Oh, and tell my baby daddy that I sent you," she said with a wink.

Damn, she hates his ass for real.

* * *

I sat in front of Zoo's mini-mansion, hoping to run into Zaryah. I had already rang the doorbell and no one came to the door, so I assumed no one was home. Lord knows I didn't wanna bump into Zoo. But if he came before her, then I was ready to go off on his ass too.

I was surprised his place wasn't gated after what happened to his crew. I mean, at least security or something. But it was easier for me, so I wasn't tripping. Zoo was a cocky nigga that thought he was bulletproof. I bet he thought security was for weak niggas.

Finally, I saw headlights coming up the long driveway. When the car got closer, I could tell it was a female. I fanned myself in the face as I prepared. For what, I didn't know. I unclicked my seatbelt and got out of the car. I didn't wanna seem weird, but I'm sure it came off that way when I met her at the doorway. She wasn't expecting anyone, so my presence spooked her.

"Detective Hollis?"

She sized me up and down and blinked her eyes repeatedly. Probably taking in my new figure. The look on her face told it. "We need to talk," I said.

She entered a code on the door and used her boy to cover it up. "Talk? At eight o'clock at night? Something ain't right with this shit." She pointed her finger up and down my body. "But you know what, I'm tired of being left out, so let's talk, Detective."

She waved me inside and I followed behind. I wanted to wrap my hands around her neck and choke her to death, but that would only catch me a charge and a death sentence from Zoo. So I played it smart and went by her lead. She still thought I was a detective.

"This is nice," I said, taking a seat in the suede sectional.

"Girl, please. Why the fuck are you really here? Because I'm at the point in my life where I don't give zero fucks right now. Ain't no cop coming over at eight o'clock at night dressed in a Fashion Nova bodysuit to do any questioning. What you looking for, Zoo? He snitching?"

What? Snitching? What the fuck is she talking about? "Snitching? I came over here to tell you that Hero is also his son and not only Hendrix," I said. Which actually sounded kinda stupid when it left my mouth.

She screwed her face up and stood up. "And why would you be—" She cut herself off. "Wait, are you fucking my nigga?"

"Been fucking him."

I closed my eyes to flip my hair then... *Boom!* "Ahhh!"

Glass shattered everywhere. That crazy bitch hit me in the head with a vase. Taking her foot, she kicked me in the chest. My body flew backward and hit the back of the sofa. She hopped on top of me and started punching me all over my head. I was bigger than her, so it was easy for me to throw her off of me.

She had caught me off guard before, but I was ready now. When I pushed her, she landed on the glass coffee table and it shattered. That bitch had pissed me off and I wanted to beat her face in. She stood up and dusted glass off of her. She had a piece of glass sticking out from her side, but I didn't give a damn. I bumrushed her and tackled her to the ground.

"AHHHHHHH!!!" she yelled out in pain. The glass in her side was now shorter than before. It had lodged deeper inside of her.

I had no sympathy for her though. I was already on top of her, so all I had to do was sit up and start giving her blow for blow. I was getting the best of her until she pulled the glass from her side and stabbed it in my back. The impact caused me to drop onto her, and she slid from under me.

She held onto her side as she slithered toward the entertainment system. She reached into a box and my entire life flashed before my eyes when I saw her point a gun at me. Not even giving me time to say anything, she fired off a shot into my head.

Pop!

CHAPTER TWENTY

ZACHARY "ZOO" SLAID

P op! *What the fuck?* The sound of a gunshot caused me to stop in my tracks as me and Hendrix were walking up to the house. Quickly, I scooped Hendrix into my arms and took him back to the car.

"Stay right here and don't fucking move," I ordered. That lil' nigga only listened if I was stern with him.

I pulled my gun from my back and hurried inside of the house. The whole time I was praying that nothing had happened to Ryah, but I was in for a fucking surprise when I opened the door.

The living room looked like a tornado ran through it. Ryah was standing up, holding her side with her left hand and holding my Glock in the right. Her face was all bruised and swollen. I followed Ryah's eyes to the side of the sofa, and Lenoir was laying there with a bullet in her skull.

"No! No! No! No! What the fuck, Ryah?"

I threw my hands to my head and took a deep breath. "FUCK!" I yelled out.

"Why the fuck did you shoot this bitch?" I was stressed. I couldn't catch a fucking break.

"Nigga, what? You worried about this bitch like I'm the one who came at her!" Ryah yelled.

"Bruh, do you not understand what you just did? This bitch was a cop and I was moving evidence from the police department through her. We got guns and drugs tucked all in her shit. The minute the cops go to her place and see all of that shit, it's gon' come back on me," I stressed.

She stood there without a care in the world. She looked me dead in the eyes and said, "Fuck you."

"What? You just caught a fucking body, Zaryah. And you acting all nonchalant. Fuck is yo' problem?" I moved my body in her direction so she couldn't get past me.

"I ain't acting like shit, Zoo. I don't give a fuck no more. I'm so tired of going through situations with niggas that ain't shit. I don't have any more tears to shed, I don't have any more feelings to process, and I don't have any fucks to give. Do what you do and make it 'disappear,'" she said.

"Am I missing something?" I stepped to her. "One minute you was begging me to get out of the streets and now you're telling me to get rid of a body? You ain't even told me what happened for real."

She was scaring me and shorty had no emotion in her face.

She shrugged. "She said something about y'all fucking around and Hero being your son too. You know, typical nigga shit."

"Ryah."

"Zoo, if you love me like you say you do, you will handle this for me and never talk to me again. You was creeping with the bitch that put me in prison. Really?"

"Let me explain, Ryah."

She kept walking past me and into the bedroom. It wasn't until I heard far-off sirens that I remembered Hendrix was in the car and I had the dead body of an ex-cop in my living room. I sent Chip a 911 text message ASAP, then I brought Hendrix in the house through the back. I didn't want him more exposed to this shit.

And I thought Ryah had really gotten to her breaking point. She was upstairs showering without a care in the world. Meanwhile, I was in the living room, dragging Lenoir's body onto the edge of the rug so I could roll her ass like a blunt.

The sounds of the sirens were getting closer, so I was moving double time. I caught hell dragging that shit to the closet. I didn't have time to properly clean, so I had to do damage control. The body and the blood was the main issue for me. And time was of the essence because I could see the blue and red lights flashing outside, but I still had a puddle of blood on my living room floor next to the sofa.

Ding. Dong. My stomach dropped to my ass. I didn't even have time to partially clean it up. I grabbed a blanket from a nearby closet and threw it on top of the blood. It soaked through so I had to grab Jase's Paw Patrol blanket on the sofa to go on top of that one.

Ding. Dong. I looked down at my clothes and I had blood on me everywhere. *Fuck.* I stripped off all my clothes and threw them in the closet with Lenoir's dead ass. I didn't have any choice but to answer the door with only some black Polo briefs.

"Can I help you with something, Officers?" I said with a fake confused look on my face. "Is my mother okay?" I added. I needed to make myself more believable.

They peeked around me, inside of the house. "Uh, we got a call from the neighbors saying they heard gunfire near your home," one of the officers spoke.

"Gunfire? I—"

But before I could finish, Ryah called out from upstairs. "Baeeee, I'm ready for round twoooo."

She caught me off guard at first, but then I picked up on what she was doing. She was trying to throw them off.

"Hold on, bae. The cops are here," I yelled back, hoping it was throwing them off.

"Cops? For what?" she yelled back.

For the fucking body you just dropped ten minutes ago. "Just go and lay back down."

I smiled. "My apologies, Officers. My lil' lady can get antsy when I'm away for too long," I joked.

I was hoping they would leave us be, but it wasn't that fucking easy. The Hannah Montana looking bitch wasn't going for it. "Do you mind if we take a look around?" she asked.

If I say no and ask for a warrant, they're gonna come back harder. Showing up with dogs and forensics. But if I tell them yeah, they can look around, see nothing, and get the fuck out. But then there's the risk of them seeing that fucking blood next to the couch.

"Ahem," I cleared my throat. "That's cool," I said, letting them inside.

"We just need to do a quick walk through to make sure nothing is out of the ordinary since we did have several calls that said the gunshot came from this house," she said.

Snitch ass neighbors. "Fasho," I said.

They looked around as they came inside, and the only thing inside my head was Ryah. I couldn't let her go down for that shit. And I couldn't kill two cops in the middle of my living room either, so the only other option I had was to take the blame. Hell, it was damn near my fault anyways, so I was willing to take that bid. Everything would be left to Skyler and the boys. And I'd put something off to the side for Ryah too.

"Got kids?" Hannah Montana asked, smiling.

I looked over and this bitch had the Paw Patrol blanket in

her hand, not even realizing the blood was on it. I rubbed my hand through my dreads and smiled nervously. "Yeah, three boys," I said.

"Awee. I have—"

Pop! Pop! Two gunshots sounded off from a distance. *My boy, Chip.* She dropped the blanket and both officers ran to the door. He started talking through the radio to the dispatcher and she rushed off to the car.

"Uh, we have to go. I'm sorry about the interruption. Enjoy the rest of your night," she said.

Talk about relief. I could finally breathe again. "Ryah!" I called out.

Nothing. "Zaryah!"

Still nothing. I made my way upstairs and she was on her way out of the bedroom with a suitcase.

"What happened to you never leaving a nigga, Ryah?" My tone was low. I knew I was wrong, so I didn't wanna push too hard.

She ignored me and continued down the stairs. And I couldn't even be mad at her 'cause she had every right to be upset. I didn't even have the time to go after her and try to make her stay. She walked through the front door and I had to let her because I had bigger shit to focus on. I had to get the dead body out of my closet and figure out how to remove all traces of us ever being in contact.

Life for me wasn't looking too good. But shit, I knew a nigga like me couldn't win forever, especially after being responsible for Maya's death. Karma spun the block one more time, and that bitch finally got me.

CHAPTER TWENTY-ONE
KAREEM "REEM" BANKS

Today was the day when everything was supposed to take place. I'd be lying if I said I wasn't nervous. Not about getting caught but about the drugs. My stomach hadn't healed all the way from Zoo's bitch ass, and now I had to swallow balloons full of drugs. One wrong move would kill my ass, and I wouldn't ever get to see my kids again. But shit, the chances of that ever happening were slim.

Geo got back with me and told me that he heard Vannah was out of prison but he hadn't heard anything about my daughter. He said that nothing had been released to the media about whether or not they had found my baby girl. I think her parents were trying to keep everything on hush because they didn't want that bad image. But fuck that, I wanted to know my kid was safe.

"Banks!" a guard called out impatiently.

Shit, I didn't even see him standing there. I had been in my cell all morning going over the plan in my head. I sent Ryah a text last night being completely honest about everything. I didn't go into details, of course, but I told her that today might be my last day living. I just really wanted her to tell my son I loved him. And I wanted her to know that I was feeling every ounce of hurt times two that I ever caused her.

She was the only one I texted though. I didn't have anybody else. My family threw me away. I mean, Geo was fucking with me a little, but that was it. I knew if my granny was in her right mind then she would be here for me too. I got both of my homeboys popped and the two women that were once crazy about me, could barely stand me.

"Banks! I'm not gon' call you again! You have a transfer and Top is waiting," he said angrily.

"Aite, chill," I said, lifting off of my bed.

He escorted me out of the cell and to the other part of the prison that led to Top. But on the way there, we passed another guard who stopped us.

"Good looking out, I was just about to grab him for visitation," he said.

"Visitation? Nah, he's a transfer and Top wants to see him before he leaves."

"Ooh, shit. Well, I'll tell his people to follow-up in the next facility."

"Nooo," I said, cutting into the conversation. "I haven't had a visitor since I've been here and I really wanna see my people. I swear it'll only take five minutes," I pleaded.

I didn't know who was here to see me, but I didn't give a damn, I just wanted to know I had some fucking body.

"Hell nah, I don't have time for this shit. Yo' ass going to Top and that's the end of it. Word around the prison is you killed one of our guys and if we find out you did, it's over. Can't nobody save you. I don't care if you're in another prison, you can still be touched," he threatened.

"Well, you gon' make time today," I heard Slug's voice from behind.

Nigga almost broke his neck to turn around and see who was trying him. Only when he saw Slug, his attitude changed quickly.

"Oh, my bad, Slug. I didn't know he—"

"Well, you know now," he said.

Damn, this nigga has it like that? He was walking the halls of the prison with no CO again, and he was ordering these niggas around like it was his prison. Oh, I had a lot to learn for real, 'cause this nigga had rank.

Slug passed me and went on to Top's office, and the original guard that was escorting me took me to my visitor. I just knew it had to be my mama. She couldn't leave her baby boy to suffer for too long, so she had to come check on me. Well, that's what I thought until I saw that I had an even better visitor. My son and Ryah.

After she told me how Jase felt about me, I thought she was going to hold off on visitation. I was glad she changed her mind.

Neither one of them looked happy to be there though. Jase was not feeling it and looked ready for a nap. Even through the raggedy piece of glass between us, Ryah was pretty as fuck like always. She had on a pink bodysuit with her half up, half down hairstyle. Big hoop earrings hung from her ears, her lips were popping from the lip gloss she wore, and she chewed gum like she didn't have a care in the world. I couldn't read her energy for shit. Was she happy to come see me or was she aggravated that she came? Either way, I was just happy that she showed up for da kid.

I put the phone to my ear and she did the same. "Thank you for bringing him," I said.

She nodded and handed Jase the phone without even saying anything to me. Her mood was cold and her eyes were even colder. Shit, I thought we were good. We were talking and texting a little, but I guess that was just that. The fact that she was pissed was obvious. Somebody had gotten on the wrong side of her. I secretly hoped it was Zoo too.

But the look in Ryah's eyes was different than the look I used to get when she was pissed off. She barely blinked.

"Hey, Daddy," Jase said, taking my attention off of Ryah.

"Ahem, hey son. How you been?" I asked.

"Good, but—" He stopped himself and looked at Ryah.

She now had tears in her eyes and she tried to look up at the ceiling to keep herself from crying.

"Let me speak to Mommy," I said, and he handed her the phone.

She rolled her eyes and placed it to her ear. "Kareem, I only came here to—"

"Your smile can brighten up any dark room. You're an amazing friend. Your personality is sexy as hell. You carry yourself like a queen. You look beautiful even when you don't try. You're the prettiest in the mornings."

"Kareem—" She tried to interrupt.

"I could have sex with you forever. You have the sweetest heart. Your cooking is amazing."

A small smirk appeared over her face. Not much, but something. "Kareem, what are you doing?"

"All I want you to do is listen, Ry. Just listen. I regret wasting your time. I was a fucking dummy. I betrayed your trust. I didn't listen, learn, or grow for you. You communicated what your needs were, and instead of trusting you, I let my own insecurities fuck up what we built... And my son..." I looked at Jase, and Ryah handed him the phone again.

"Always respect your mama. Daddy didn't do it right, but I know you can. I'm sorry for messing up, son. I love you," I said.

The tear that was hanging onto the side of my face dropped, and I had to wipe it before anyone saw. You couldn't show any signs of weakness in this bitch. I didn't have any other choice but to stay strong. I was lowkey pissed because this nigga Zoo was out here doing my baby mama wrong. I could see it all in her face. And I knew I couldn't be one to talk when I took her through hell and back, but I saw shit differently now.

Ryah never had shit easy. She lost her parents at a young age. Luckily, she had Kamara and her mother when she grew up in the system. Then I came along and fucked up her life some more. I knew she was weak and didn't know what real love was, so I took advantage of it. She loved a nigga through everything. She didn't know how to let go, until she met Zoo. And his ass bragged about taking my bitch only to do her dirty. Foul ass nigga.

"Thank you for saying those things, Reem." She smiled a little more.

"I think we're both afraid of the same thing... being alone. Even though I was a dumb ass nigga, I know you for real. And the woman I know deserves everything she wants. I know you want a nice house on the hills with little babies running around. You want a man that can provide, lay the wood, and love you everywhere you need it. You deserve better than me. You deserve better than him. Get you a lawyer or a doctor. Hell, maybe an architect or an astronaut. Shit, you deserve it. You deserve more than just a street nigga with money. Go and start your life over. Be free from this shit. And I have just the plan for y'all. I'll have an account with fifty grand in it in a few days. I'm doing jobs here and every time I finish my end of the deal, I get paid. I know you probably don't want dirty money, but it's enough to start y'all off with."

"Look at you, trying to take care of us. I appreciate you, Kareem. I'mma take what you said into consideration. And despite all of what we've been through, one minute I can hate yo' ass, but I'll always have love for you. Until next time, baby daddy." She stood to her feet and they left.

And I was back to it.

* * *

"Do you remember everything we told you?" Top asked, standing over me.

"Yeah, I got it. What I'm concerned about is the time. How long do I have before these balloons start to burst inside of me?" I countered.

"I don't know, nigga. Stick to the plan and you won't have to worry about that," he barked.

"Yeah, aite."

I stood to my feet so I could go to the transfer van. I couldn't believe I had to swallow twenty-seven balloons of cocaine. I will say that it came with some luxuries. I had to spend the rest of my life in that shit hole, so I might as well make the best of it. These niggas at the top of the ranks were living good here. Slug had life made and I wanted that same respect and power he had.

So I took my ass to that van to carry out the plan. Slug had already told me the more work you put in, the better you come out. I was hungry for change in life, so I manned up and put all of my fears behind me. When I could get around to it, I planned to see if Slug could pull a few strings and find out any information on my daughter.

But the first thing was survival. I went over the plan in my head over and over for the whole two hours. I didn't wanna miss any steps 'cause I had two obstacles against me. If I took too long, I'd be dead before sundown and if I got caught, they was gon' put a nigga in solitary for life. I couldn't miss any key points. Every box had to be checked.

They escorted me and two other niggas off of the van and we went into a room to be strip searched. It's the most embarrassing shit ever. I couldn't even get into it. As the time went by, the more anxious I got. I had to wait until we got to in-processing to set everything off.

You'll ask to go to the bathroom. One of the guards will escort you. Once you get inside, the second stall on the left has a vent above the toilet. Get 'em out and put them inside. Slug's words replayed inside of my head over and over. As soon as I got a minute, I asked the guard if I could go to the bathroom.

"You got three minutes," he said.

He escorted me to the bathroom like Slug said, and he waited outside the door. I was still cuffed around my ankles and my hands, so he wasn't worried about me trying anything funny. What he didn't know was, I was carrying a load worth more than his salary in my stomach.

Stepping into the bathroom, I immediately went to the second stall on the left to rid my body of that shit before I overdosed. This nigga said I had three minutes, so I didn't have time to lollygag. I took my fingers and placed them down my throat.

One by one the balloons dropped to the floor. They were hitting the ground loud as fuck, so I had to crouch down so they wouldn't make too much noise. Every time a balloon traveled through my throat, I felt like I couldn't breathe and had to beat my chest to give myself an extra push.

The guard knocked on the door to tell me to speed up, but I only had thirteen balloons out. That put the fire under my ass because I wasn't coming out until all twenty-seven were out. I gagged and hacked until I was able to finish getting them all. And the guard came in right after I stepped down from the toilet.

"What are you doing, inmate? Let's go," he ordered.

I hurried my ass out of the stall and to the sink.

"I been holding that shit for two hours," I said.

I only said that to throw him off. He ignored me and we went back to in-processing. Damn, I was relieved. I was proud of myself too. I didn't think I could pull that shit off. Heh, these niggas in trouble. I was in the process of becoming a self-made American gangster.

CHAPTER TWENTY-TWO
SAVANNAH GOOD
1 MONTH LATER

"Good session today!" I yelled out to my therapist as I rushed out of her office.

I looked down at my cell phone, seeing I had an hour to get to work and Atlanta's traffic was the worst. Especially when you have to take Ubers everywhere you go. Since getting out of jail, I changed my life around tremendously. For starters, I decided to listen to my parents and get the help I needed from professionals. I went to therapy once a week to talk about my issues. And I also saw a psychiatrist. She had me on medication to help me sleep and antidepressants. And I had to admit, I'd been feeling much better.

I got a job at a call center two weeks ago. The money wasn't that great, but it felt good to get out of the house and have a purpose. Daddy saw me getting better too, so he decided it was time for him to move out and give me some space. My parents had been extremely supportive through everything. They hadn't let me see Blessing yet, but I'd been working on that too. I was finding myself again, slowly, but it was coming.

Bzzt. Bzzt. Bzzt. I pulled my phone out of my purse and saw that my mama was Facetime-ing me. I dragged my thumb across the screen to answer. And there she was, the cutest little baby in the world.

"Hey, Snooka Butt. You look so pretty." I made kissing noises through the phone "Mommy loves you! Mommy loves you," I said.

I had my phone up to my face, not paying attention to where I was going, and I ran into a dude crossing the road with a cane. He went falling forward and my phone dropped out of my hand and fell into the sewer drain.

"FUCK!" I yelled out.

I didn't pay him any mind, I was worried about my phone. I had just gotten that phone and it wasn't cheap.

"Damn, you worried about a phone and I'm over here on the ground," I heard him say.

I turned around on level ten. My eyes peered at him through tight slits. "You made my damn phone fall into the sewer," I spat.

He raised one of his thick eyebrows and licked his lips. I put my hand behind my neck and turned to look away. He was trying to be cute and even though he was, I wasn't falling for it.

"You got life fucked up... But I've always had a soft spot for a pretty face, so I'll pay for another phone when you help me up," he said.

Now I was standing there looking stupid because I didn't expect him to do that. And I damn sure didn't think he would compliment me. And shit, he wasn't too bad looking himself. He gave me bad boy vibes. I extended my hand out to him and grabbed a hold.

Picture my little ass trying to pull up a man twice my size. We got it done though. He did most of the work. I wanted to be nosy and ask him what happened to him, but I didn't wanna impose. It just shocked me to see a man as fine as him on a cane. And I'd be his nurse any day. It's crazy how I went from hopping down his throat to undressing him with my eyes within thirty seconds.

After he stood to his feet, I remembered the time. "Can I use your phone to call for an Uber?" I asked.

"Nah, I got you. Let me give you a ride. I already owe you a phone. We can stop by the Verizon store and I can get you a phone," he said.

"Oh, you were serious?"

"I don't have a reason to lie." I looked around nervously and smiled.

"I have to get to work, so I don't have time," I said.

"No problem, I'll drop you off and give you the money for you to take care of it later," he said.

"Fuck it," I said. "I work at Citron in East Atlanta. On 44th," I continued.

"Got you."

And just like that, I was in the car with a fine ass stranger. I was finally taking a chance like my therapist had been suggesting. She wanted me to add some type of mystery or fun to my life because I had become such a robot.

And it actually felt good to let my guard down and just enjoy the moment. He had the music blasting with the air blasting. We didn't say anything to each other. He drove and bobbed his head to Lil' Durk.

I was in my own little world, playing with the ends of my braids. Before I knew it, we were pulling up in the parking lot of my job. He reached into the armrest and pulled out a stack of money. It was marked 1K.

"Take that and get a new phone. And I don't wanna come off rude but damn, you are beautiful. And I know it's soon, but would you mind keeping me company after you get off?" he asked.

I paused. *Is this nigga really trying me and he has only known me all of thirty minutes?* "Uh, you don't even know me," I said.

"That's why I'm trying to get to know you."

"No, you're trying to fuck," I countered. I might've been crazy a few weeks ago, but I was still woman enough to know when a nigga wanted pussy.

"Shit, I would love to. I really just wanted the company, but the pussy is always a plus. And please forgive me if this comes off as offensive to you, but I'm willing to pay for it."

Snapping my neck at him, I couldn't believe my ears. I sat up in my seat, ready to go off on him, but then he put his hand on my knee.

"It's no disrespect to you. So before you hype up and snap on a nigga, calm down. I know you're not that type of girl. I can look at you and tell. That's why I want it. And I can't sit up here and lie. I ain't felt pussy since I got popped up. Every bitch looks at me and feels sorry for me. I can't stand that shit. But yo' ass didn't give a fuck. You came at me raw and I'm matching yo' vibe, for real. And when I say I'll pay for it, I don't mean some lil' chump change. I got fifty on it. And I'm talking fifty grand," he said.

Fifty grand?! For some pussy? Well, my therapist did want me to be a little more spontaneous. "I get off at seven," I said, opening the door. "And my name is Savannah."

"I'm Romeo. Romeo Walton."

CHAPTER TWENTY-THREE
SKYLER SINCLAIR

Day so hard, so much stress
Life won't let up, boy just rest
Lay down and let me cover you in all these kisses
So much on your mind, it weighs on your head
But baby you're worry free in this bed
Go 'head and let me cover you in all these kisses

I sang Tammy Rivera's "All These Kisses" to the top of my lungs as I pulled into Ms. Irene's driveway to meet Zoo. We'd been meeting here to swap off the kids for the past month to keep down the arguing and fighting. And to my surprise, me and my baby daddy actually had gotten along a little better.

Me and Hero moved closer to Hendrix and Zoo a week ago. I must say, everything had been working out for us. No arguments or fights. And then I hadn't heard from that Lenoir girl since she popped up at my condo. Which I'm sure my baby daddy took care of her dumb ass. She was shot the fuck out.

But what's crazy was, I picked up on the vibe that he and

Ryah weren't together anymore. He didn't speak on it, but I could tell by his mood. That man was lost and he had a sadness in him that even his children couldn't fill. He hid it well, but he had lost his true love and those who knew him well could see it.

Even after how badly I showed my ass before, I still felt bad for him. I realized long ago that I was being childish and let go of the petty beef I was holding onto. We never apologized to each other or anything. We just kinda let it wash over with time.

Opening the door, I got out of the car to get the boys. Hendrix gave Zoo dap and Hero gave him a hug.

` "I love y'all," he said. "Be good for your mama," he continued.

They ran over to me and Hero jumped into my arms. "Don't leave just yet," I called out to my baby daddy.

He walked over to my car as the boys climbed inside. "What's up?" he asked.

"I'm going on vacation for a week with my friend. So Hero is gonna have to stay with you or my mama for that week," I said.

"Oh, a friend, huh?" He laughed. "I had a friend and you opened the gates of Hell on me," he joked.

I playfully rolled my eyes. "Whatever."

"Nah, for real though. You know my boys are welcome anytime. And with all the hell you put me through, I kinda deserved it. I had a lot of time to think this past month. It ain't easy raising children and although I was there financially, it would've made an even bigger difference if I was present. I knew why you were mad, I just didn't know how to fix it. Other than being the father that they deserved. You were hard on me and I'm glad you were, because it taught me to step up my shit big time. I learned to become a father quickly. Me and you had a rough start but we don' came a long way. And if I never said it before, I wanna make it known today. You are a very important person in my life. You are my kids' mother. You will always be protected and well off. Any woman that comes into my life will never come before my kids. You gotta hear me on that shit. I'd risk it all for you and my boys. They'll always need their mother before they need a nigga like me."

He pulled me into a hug, with my crybaby ass. Zoo had never expressed himself to me that way, ever. I always thought he regretted getting me pregnant and he only took care of us because he knew it was his responsibility. He actually had love for me.

"I am so sorry, Zoo."

"Nah, we good for real, ma. Don't cry." He raised my chin and flashed his slugs.

I pulled away from his chest. "I don't know if you know this, but some Lenoir lady came by here asking questions about you, and I told her about Hero. It was only to get payback at you. I shouldn't have done that. I was so fucking mad that I just wanted you to hurt as bad as I hurt," I let out.

"Word? I don't know how that crazy bitch got information on me and mine. I took care of that though. That's old news."

"Why were you fucking that woman when you claimed you loved Zaryah so much?"

"Man, I love Zaryah to death. I only fucked that bitch to keep my homie out them cages. I cut her ass off and she went fucking dumb. Bitch changed her whole identity to be like Ryah. The only reason I had continued strings with her is because I got tied up into drugs and guns with her. But yeah, she's long gone along with every piece of evidence of her being tied to me. It cost me a pretty penny to cover this shit up. I needed help with this one," he said.

I was surprised as to how comfortable he was to tell me

something so personal. We were really co-parenting and trusting one another. "Wow, that's crazy. How is Romeo? Has he gotten better?" I pried.

"Ro?" He smiled and shook his head. "He's been doing good. Going to physical therapy three times a week at the hospital. And he uses a cane to walk with. But to be honest, we just started back hanging. He said he wanted space after we had differences. We just recently started talking again. I wasn't tripping 'cause I knew he needed space. He's always been like that. When he's hurt, he likes to be alone. And what's up with all the questions?" He folded his arms across his chest.

"I just wanted to make sure that you were good since you and Zaryah aren't together anymore. I see the difference with you, baby daddy."

He shrugged. "Everything don't last forever, baby mama."

"You know what you have to do to get that woman back. So whatever it is, I hope you do it. My sons wanna see their father happy. Show them how to treat a woman and how a woman is supposed to be loved. It's not too late, Zoo."

I never saw myself saying those words, but before I knew it, they were coming out of my mouth. I could tell he needed to hear it too. He hugged me so tight then he jumped into his car and took off.

CHAPTER TWENTY-FOUR
ZACHARY "ZOO" SLAID

Damn, me and baby mama never had a heart to heart like that. Shit felt good to know that our relationship had come to a healthy point. She threw me off with the Lenoir situation, but it wasn't that big of a deal to trip about. That situation was taken care of and that was that.

But she fucked me up for real when she brought up Ryah. That was a face that I was trying to push to the back of my head. Ever since we called it quits a month ago, a nigga's chest been hurting. Shit hadn't felt the same without her and Jase around the house. The boys asked about them all the time too.

I blew her phone up the first week she left, and she soon blocked me from her phone and all social media. Which didn't matter 'cause I had Symone look her up for me the next week. I saw that she was living with Kamara's OG and she had opened up a shoe boutique in Kennesaw.

The first week she opened, I bought half of her inventory online. I had several pairs of shoes shipped to the girls at the salon. I told them to go crazy and get any type of shoes they wanted. Every time I saw Symone for the past month, I couldn't help but ask her to pull up Ryah's page just so I could check on her. She always looked happy in everything that she did. She never looked like what she had been through.

She was living life content, without me. I didn't wanna bother her with my bullshit if she was happy, but Sky got in my head for real. I hadn't been the same man since Ryah left. I was good for the most part but truthfully, I was just going through the motions.

I don't know how many times I'd wished that Ryah would just come back. I was hoping I had got her ass pregnant and she would come back and tell me or some shit, but the longer I waited for her, the more I realized she wasn't coming back. And Sky was right. The only thing that would get my girl back was getting out of these fucking streets.

It had already been a thought on my mind, but I just couldn't see myself going the clean route. I don't know what the fuck I was scared of, but hearing Sky tell me that shit felt like a sign. Instead of going home and playing the game like I had planned, I headed to my main bank.

On my way there, I had to call the homies and let 'em in on my new life changes. Romeo felt my pain and said he had been thinking about doing the same. When he lost Kamara, it was a game changer for him. We had a conversation about my new addition too, and he was shocked just like I was.

And Chip, my soldier, still had a taste for the street life. We decided to pass everything to him. As long as we still had somebody to run the empire, muthafuckas didn't care who the face was.

And as for me, I had the bank teller set me up with the best investments that my business broker suggested. I had more than enough money to retire on but wanted to keep the generational wealth going. So I told the bank that I had money that I wanted to make money, and the teller set me up with a broker.

I didn't know much about investments, but she walked me through everything and made it pretty simple for a high-class street nigga. Surprisingly, it already felt like weights were being lifted from my shoulders. Putting my money into something legit felt good. I felt accomplished and I actually didn't feel like a menace to society for once.

Taking out my phone, I went to the messages and sent Kamara's mother a text, asking her for a favor. I knew it was weird for her to see my number pop across the screen, but a young nigga needed help.

CHAPTER TWENTY-FIVE
ZARYAH "RYAH" COX

"I just can't believe the store is doing so well," I said, sticking a label onto yet another shoe box. "I was prepared for a slow take off, but my website did numbers and the store wasn't so bad either. I didn't even think that many people knew about it either," I said.

Ms. Wade slapped her hand on her hip and stood to her feet. "Honey, aren't you happy about that? Why does it sound like you're complaining? You've spent the last month burying your head into this boutique so you can take your mind off of Zoo, and now you still can't find happiness," she fussed.

"Ma—I meant, Ms.—"

"No. No. It's okay, Ryah. I don't mind it," she said.

"I didn't mean to. It just happened, I guess."

She smiled with tears in her eyes. She reached her hands out to me. "Come, I want to show you the house I bought with the insurance money from Kamara's death. It's much bigger, for me, you, and Jase," she said.

I fixed my face to tell her no, but she beat me to the refusal. "I'm not taking no for an answer," she said.

"I look a mess and I still have more shoes to box up," I said, hoping she would excuse me. I hadn't had much energy to do anything but focus on my son and my business. I literally hadn't indulged in anything else.

"Girl, put some shoes on and come on. These shoes can wait for a few hours," she fussed.

"Okayyy," I sighed.

I slid my feet into my bunny bedroom slippers next to the couch. I still had on my pajamas at noon. But that was because the time slipped past me this morning when I was labeling boxes.

"I'm wearing this," I said.

She shrugged. "As long as you come, I'm good."

I dragged myself to the car, not wanting to go. Ms. Wade was right. I had been trying to avoid thoughts about Zoo, but it was hard. The first week, he blew up my phone, explaining to me what went down between him and Lenoir. I didn't believe that shit. But I got a sign from friend telling me to interrogate the homeboy. Not Romeo but Chip. He was sweet, and I knew he kept it real with me. He told me everything that Zoo told me. I just never went back to Zoo because I was truly done with him.

We got into the car and we drove the entire ride listening to Aretha Franklin and the Braxton Sisters. It wasn't my cup of tea, but the ride was short so it didn't bother me much. We pulled into a long driveway, up a hill to the most beautiful house I had ever seen.

I was starstruck, shocked from the perfection. The grounds were beautiful, decorated with gardens and flowers all around. The house resembled the modern barnyard effect. The wrap-around porch was my all-time favorite.

"I-I-I love it," I said. I was so excited, I couldn't wait for Ms.

Wade. I was eager to see the inside. I burst the doors open and got the surprise of my life.

The lights were dimmed, rose petals led to the kitchen, and my favorite song played lowly on the surround sound.

Yours, mine, ours
I could do this for hours
Sit and talk to you for hours
I wanna give you your flowers
And some champagne showers
Order shrimp and lobster towers
But it's me that gets devoured
Ooh, when you do what you do, I'm empowered
You give me a superpower
Together the world could be ours
You sit me up on the counter
Instantly, it's thunder showers
Stormin' for a couple hours
When we finished, take a shower

I followed the rose petals to the kitchen and an involuntary smile crossed my face. There was a glass of wine set on the table along with a single rose, a key, and a letter.

Dear Zaryah, I didn't know what becoming a man meant until I met you. The woman that you are encouraged me to be a better man. Because of you, I've accomplished more with things I never saw myself doing. Our entire time of knowing each other, you've always wanted better for me. You always knew my potential but I could never see it in myself. I'm sorry for never seeing it before, but I see it now. Love is the bigger picture. I love you and my sons with everything in me, and that includes Jase as well. For y'all, I'd risk it all. And I did. You are now looking at a man that is removing himself from the streets. I'm tired of doing the back and forth, one minute I love you, one minute I hate you thing. I wanna be good with you and have your love forever. I wanna be tied in with you for life.

A tear dropped from my eye onto the letter and when I looked up, my heart skipped a beat. He stood there in a white wife beater, grey sweatpants, and some Nike socks. Looking like he just knew I was gon' take him back.

"Can a nigga please have one more chance?"

I walked over to him and smashed my lips into his. Our tongues danced around passionately, then we parted. "This shit with us forever. Don't you ever forget that."

The End

...